j

C. l

Levitin, Sonia
    Silver days.   Atheneum, 1989.
    [186] p.
    Sequel to: Journey to America.

I. Title.

 88-27491/13.95/1189

Books by Sonia Levitin

Silver Days

Silver Days

by Sonia Levitin

j

C . l

ATHENEUM   1989   NEW YORK

Atheneum
Macmillan Publishing Company
866 Third Avenue, New York, NY 10022
Collier Macmillan Canada, Inc.
First Edition   Printed in the United States of America

10 9 8 7 6 5 4 3 2 1

Library of Congress Cataloging-in-Publication Data
Levitin, Sonia.
    Silver days/by Sonia Levitin.—1st ed. p. cm.
    Summary: Escaping from Hitler's Germany, a prosperous Jewish
family lives in a New York City tenement until Papa decides
to move the family to California.
    ISBN 0-689-31563-5
    [1. Emigration and immigration—Fiction. 2. Jews—United States
—Fiction. 3. German Americans—Fiction. 4. World War, 1939–1945—
United States—Fiction.] I. Title. PZ7.L58Sg 1989
[Fic]—dc19   88–27491   CIP   AC

IN MEMORY OF MY BELOVED SISTER VERA,
AND FOR MY SISTER EVA,
WITH LOVE.

Chapter I

WE WERE TOGETHER AGAIN with Papa. While we were
separated, I'd wished and prayed for this every day. People
always think that when a wish comes true everything will
be perfect; it never is.

Mother, Annie, Ruth, and I had waited a whole year
in Switzerland for Papa to send for us. None of us realized
it would take so long. In fact, when we finally did see
Papa again, Annie didn't recognize him. She was only
three when Papa left Germany in secret, escaping the Nazis.

On the ship to America everybody had a story to tell.
Most people were fleeing from Europe because, as they
said, war was in the wind. Mother told our story again
and again during that rough sea voyage, as if by telling it
she could at last realize we were on the way to freedom.

I thought continually about America, how it would be
to live there. On the ship we saw American movies, with
brightly dressed people living in beautiful houses. People

sang a lot in those movies, and danced. I dreamed of dancing, too, in America.

At the dock Papa kissed us all, and it was so exciting! Papa was wearing a woolen suit and a hat. He said some words to the bus driver in English. How we marveled! Papa was so American! We thought he must be rich. I expected to see a pretty white house with a red-tile roof, grass out front, and a weather vane. But when I saw the apartment, I could hardly believe it. The place smelled of grease and green soap and stray cats. The stairs were treacherously uneven. Mother said we were never to loiter in the dark halls.

The streets echoed with the noise of peddlers and screaming housewives, clattering carts, and huge trucks with their harsh horns. Ragged underclothes flapped on lines strung between the tenements; refuse from rusty cans burst out onto the alleyways, where little kids played and the older boys hung around, acting tough.

Annie was too young to be out on the street alone. Ruth couldn't be bothered with Annie, so she became my shadow.

Strange, how suddenly we had become poor. And it seemed I was the only one who really minded.

I vowed, somehow, to make things better for myself and my family. I began by doing little jobs for people in the building. I took out the trash for old Mrs. Zlnotnik and plunked a dime a week into my bank, which was an empty glass jar, carefully sealed and slotted on top. I babysat for the Morellis for twenty cents an hour. I saved my money, and on Sundays I took Annie on the bus and dragged her beside me along Fifth Avenue, where we peered into shop windows and dreamed.

When I caught glimpses of myself in the large plateglass windows, I was startled. In my imagination I was a fine lady off to the furrier's or the jewelry store with her lovely little girl. In the window I saw myself as a thin thirteen-year-old girl wearing a bulky dark-blue coat, a ragged muffler, and an almost-fierce expression. So here I was in America, lonely and miserable, and feeling guilty, too, because I wasn't satisfied. I longed for the pretty things in the shop windows. I longed for some gentle, interesting friends.

My only friend was Essie Cantor, who lived a block away in a tenement just like ours. Essie walked to school with us, and sometimes she came over. But, really, she wasn't any fun. There were a thousand things she wasn't allowed to do, because her family was so religious. Papa said they were a "little crazy—so *fromm* they hardly dared to breathe the air." *Fromm* is a German word that means "holy." We used a lot of German words; English stuck on our tongues.

For the first few months we had no furniture except beds. Papa found orange crates somewhere, with the faded labels still on them. I remember one of them, a picture of green hills, blue sky, and, in the foreground, a lovely young woman all in blue, holding an armful of blossoms. CALIFOR-NIA ORANGES! said the sticker, and the young woman smiled in the sunshine.

We made seats of the orange crates, using an old card table given to us by a Jewish lady Papa had met, Mrs. Morgenstrom. Mrs. Morgenstrom had helped Papa get the visa so he could send for us. She was like a queen in our home. Mama and Papa would hear nothing against her, though she had her peculiarities, like everyone else. Mrs. Morgenstrom never stopped talking. It was like diarrhea of the mouth, Papa said, but privately, to me only.

I don't know where Mrs. Morgenstrom got the things

she brought us, but we'd hear her panting up the stairs, then a thump and a knock, then a large carton would be pushed into the room, and she would begin, "My dears, have a look at this."

We would gather around the box, breathless and waiting. My mother would open it, and out would come things like blankets, pillows, clothes, and shoes, all cast-off and dingy, but to us, priceless.

After we'd been in New York for a couple of months, Mrs. Morgenstrom brought the card table. There was a hole in the top; you could see several layers of gray felt down to the metal. One leg bent sideways, so that the table leaned.

"It doesn't matter," Mama said, mildly. "We're together. That's what counts."

The clothes smelled funny. We washed them, but they still looked wrong. I had two dresses, one a blue-and-white-striped dress with a black patent-leather belt. This was my favorite, and I wore it to school three days a week, alternating it with a beige wool dress. The clothes hung on me strangely. Luckily, in the box I had found a yellow artificial rose. Sometimes I pinned it to my dress, sometimes I wore it in my hair.

I longed to be sixteen, like Ruth, or even fourteen. By then, I hoped, my hair would have found its true color, a rich auburn. Now, it was an indistinct pale brown. My face was covered with freckles, and with my large blue-gray eyes, I was sure I was the ugliest girl in the entire world. The yellow artificial rose made me feel, if not pretty, at least grand.

The first semester in New York, Ruth and I took a special English class for an hour each day during school. After that, we were on our own. Ruth made great strides; she had already studied English in Germany. But for me, it was very hard.

I tried to be like the other kids, laughing and making plans. I didn't feel excited, the way the other kids seemed to; besides, I always had to get home to take care of Annie. The strange cafeteria food made me sick—chili, beets, and corn dogs. It seemed that I could never fit in, except at home with Papa.

Papa and I were alike; he loved nice things, too, and like me, he was a dreamer. I made him laugh with my monkey faces and impersonations. Sometimes I danced for him, and he applauded, "Bravo!" He said, "Someday you will be a famous ballerina, dancing all over the world! Then, will you take care of your old papa?"

Mother shook her head as she padded around from kitchen to table in her old felt slippers. I knew she was thinking that I ought to have dancing lessons, as I'd had in Germany. Dancing lessons! Might as well wish for the moon.

"Arthur, Arthur," she sighed, "please don't fill the child's head with impossible hopes."

Papa laughed. "Nothing is impossible. Look where we are! Listen, Henry Ford started out poor, making a car in a shed. He was so poor, he didn't even own the shed! Look where he is today! A multimillionaire. That's America."

"Is it possible, in America, to get a light bulb in the bathroom?" Mama asked dryly.

"You know it's bad wiring, Margo, and not the bulb," he retorted.

"I know everything," Mama said, closing her eyes. Lately she had this way of closing her eyes for long moments at a time, blotting things out. Her hands were always red and chapped. Mama worked as a scrubwoman in a restaurant;

sometimes the owner gave her day-old bread to bring home, and on rare occasion, a big sour pickle.

She had changed, too, here in America. Once gentle and eternally patient, my mother had become more brittle, like a comb that snaps and breaks when you try to pull it through your hair. Little things set her off unreasonably, I thought.

One night at supper I said, "My teacher told us to take a bath every day and to keep our towels and brushes strictly to ourselves."

Ruth looked up. "Who wants to use your towel anyway?"

"Don't start," said my father. He wore a threadbare white dress shirt with the sleeves rolled up to hide the holes in the elbows. All day he walked through the garment district with a large peddler's case strapped to his back. He sold neckties. In Germany Papa had prospered as a manufacturer of ladies' coats.

"I'm not starting," said Ruth. "But she's always coming home with stories of what we have to do. Since when is Lisa's teacher our boss?"

"I like taking a bath," said Annie, giving me a smile.

"Also," I continued, "my teacher said we must eat foods from certain groups."

"Groups?" repeated my mother, ladling out potatoes and green beans, which swam in a greasy sauce. "What is this child talking about? What kind of a school is it where children are taught to tell their parents what to do?"

"It is America," Papa murmured. He smiled proudly. That very day he had brought us chairs from the thrift shop. "Forty-five cents apiece, they cost," he told us. "You see? America!"

"Food groups," I continued, undaunted. "We should eat green vegetables, grains, fruits, eggs or cheese or milk, and meat every day. . . ."

With pursed lips my mother passed the bread, warped, dark slices for mopping up the gravy. We'd had a piece of lamb days ago. Now all that was left was the gravy, and Mother frowning over it.

"Pass the pickles," said my father. "Please." He gave me a cautionary look. I ignored it.

"People can't stay healthy unless they eat the right foods," I said. "In my cooking class at school . . ."

"Do they say anything at school," my mother snapped, "about children helping to clean up after the meal? Without a fight? Do they talk about that, too?" Her hands were balled into fists, propped at the table's edge.

"We always do the dishes," I argued.

Annie kept swirling the beans around on her plate.

Ruth's eyes were large and dark. Her full mouth was set, stern. Unlike me, she was a beauty. "May I be excused?" Ruth said. "I have homework to do, and I hate talking about baths and food groups and all that. Some people know how to make pleasant conversation at the table."

She turned, giving me a cold glance. The thin, shabby curtains, the shadowy light from our single lamp, the cracked dishes at our table all seemed to contrast and emphasize Ruth's steadfast beauty. I felt stung, breathless.

"Listen, Ruth," I said, "just because you're sixteen doesn't mean you know everything. Nobody does. Not even grown-ups."

My mother pulled back from the table, tossing her napkin down. "Is this what they learn here in America?" she cried. "Disrespect to parents? Imagine if I had said such things to my parents. . . ."

"The child meant no disrespect," said Papa, quickly rising to go to her.

"Mama, I am only trying to teach you . . . !"

"Since when do children teach parents?" my mother cried, trembling. She pushed at Papa as he vainly patted her back. "Every day you come home with something and always it costs money. What do you think I am doing all day in that restaurant? Drinking coffee? Eating cream puffs? Look at my hands!"

"Mama, I only meant . . ."

Annie crept from her seat, trailed down the hall to our room.

"Enough!" my father cried. "Never again do I want to hear what your teacher says."

"Papa!" Ruth gasped, for we had always been taught to respect our teachers.

"You know what I mean!" he thundered. "Now, into the kitchen, all of you, Annie, too. Everything clean—dishes, floor, and also the stove. Half an hour from now I am making an inspection. For shame, making your mother cry."

Ruth was furious. "Look what you've done. You'll wash."

Usually I would have protested or at least insisted on tossing a coin. This night I bowed my head, filled the basin with soapy water, and began to wash, hating my big mouth, my awkwardness at school, my loneliness. I had not told what else my teacher had said today. Maybe then they would have felt sorry for me.

Later, in bed, I whispered it to Ruth. "My teacher said

I was stupid because I didn't know what she meant when she told us to go to the lavatory. She said it in front of the whole class.''

"You didn't know what lavatory means?'' Ruth sounded amazed.

"What a dumb language!'' I raged. "Why do they have so many words for the same thing? Bathroom, toilet, rest room, and now lavatory. We've been here almost a year, and still . . .''

"They also call it the john,'' Ruth said.

"What? You're joking.''

"It's true.''

I waited a few minutes, then got up out of bed and lit the candle I always kept on the windowsill. By the flickering light I wrote in my little red diary.

September 19, 1940. Today the teacher called me stupid. I was shaking so terribly I thought I might faint. But I forced myself to go numb. Not to listen. Not to see. It was like that time in Germany, when the teacher called me up to the front of the class and said, "Look at this Jewish pig, children! I don't want to see any of you talking to her.''

I paused. Ought such memories be saved? For a moment I thought of ripping the page out. Then I added,

But this is America. It is different here. We left the war behind us in Germany.

I got back into bed and quickly said the *Shema*. Mama usually came into our room at night to say it with us. Tonight, I supposed, she was just too tired.

The next morning before school I rushed to make another
entry in my little book:

*Mother is still mad at me this morning, but Papa gave
me one of the neckties that is frayed. I am going to
wear it!*

Chapter 2

MOTHER AND PAPA attended night school twice a week. They also had a little book of questions about government, which they studied over and over again, and Papa tried to impress the teacher, Mrs. "Tatcher."

"Mrs. Tatcher says I am learning the Constitution so good I can give lessons."

"Thatcher," I corrected him. "So *well*, not *good.*"

"So, it's good for me, I'm learning, isn't it?"

"Mrs. Tatcher says Roosevelt will win the election," Papa said excitedly after class one night in November. It was election day, 1940. "Three terms! The first time in the history of the United States that a president will be in for three terms."

Mother made tea. It was a celebration of sorts.

"They are still counting the ballots," she told us. "But Roosevelt is winning." Her eyes shone. She loved the president.

"It's because of the war in Europe," Ruth said. "My teacher told us about it. People don't want to change presidents in wartime."

"We're not in the war," I said. I hated such talk. At school the teachers said we should read the newspapers, and they pointed to the large map of Europe, showing how the Germans had seized Holland, Czechoslovakia, Austria, Poland, and now France.

But America was far away from all that. America was bounded by two great oceans. Didn't I know it! We had crossed the Atlantic Ocean, and it was huge.

Mama patted my hand. "That's right, Lisa," she said. "We are safe here. Especially with President Roosevelt. And he will let our people in."

Papa took a sip of tea, dunked in a piece of zwieback, and ate it with pleasure. "President Roosevelt is a real democrat. A wealthy man," he said, looking around at us, making his point, "but a great friend of the poor, the oppressed."

I asked, "Does this mean Grandmother will come to us?"

Mother's eyes became red rimmed. She turned away. Ruth gave me a dark look.

"Why couldn't Grandma come to America with us?" Annie cried. "Why did we leave her?"

"Hush up, Annie," Ruth muttered.

"You know we wanted to bring her," Mama said in a low voice. "She couldn't leave. Said she couldn't . . ."

"We will do everything humanly possible," Papa said.

"I know, Arthur," Mother said. She blinked rapidly.

We had heard nothing from Grandmother for months. The last letter had been censored, with thick, dark lines blotting out words the Nazis did not want people to read. Often, we knew, they arrested people for speaking out against them. "But they wouldn't arrest a seventy-five-year-old woman," my mother had said staunchly, though nobody could be sure.

"We're doing everything we can," Papa said. "We've sent documents to the consul, references . . . Look, with Roosevelt in the White House for another term, she'll be all right. Roosevelt won't let Hitler have his way. He'll send supplies to England—planes, food, guns. Roosevelt won't dodge war when it means liberty. . . ."

"War, war, war!" I cried. "That's all you ever talk about!"

Papa stared at me. For a moment I thought he'd be very angry. Then, softly, he said, "You're right, Lisa. We have to live for today, not always worrying. Listen, I have something fine to tell you. Today," he said, "I sold ten neckties, all to the same man. A prince," Papa proclaimed. Papa knew two categories of people: a man was a prince or a crook.

"Arthur, who needs ten ties all at once?"

Papa chuckled, glancing at me. He reached into his pocket, took out the photographs he kept of us, and laid them out in a row. "Maybe he didn't need ten ties," Papa said. "But I showed him these."

"Good people," Mother murmured, smiling again.

"And I have a special job Friday night," Papa continued.

"What? Nobody works on Friday nights," Mother said.

Some Friday nights, in Germany, we had gone to the temple. I remembered the candles shining, and how the rabbi spoke about living a noble life, a life with meaning, with Torah. Afterward we had wonderful refreshments in

the social hall. Now, we had not been to temple in several
years.

"Look, in America, if you want to survive, you work,"
replied my father. "And for the night's work I am getting
ten dollars."

"Ten dollars!" Ruth gasped. "What do you have to
do, Papa? Rob a bank?"

Papa laughed. "Not at all. In fact, I'll wear a fine black
suit and a stiff white shirt. Maybe even gloves."

"I knew it!" Ruth cried, laughing. "You're going to
crack a safe."

"No. I'm going to be a waiter. My friend Manny Freed-
man works as a waiter for banquets. On weekends. One
of the waiters is in the hospital. Manny said I can fill in.
Ten dollars for a night's work. Not bad, is it?" He grinned.
"That's America."

Mother shook her head. "That's a lot of money," she
said.

"I'll buy you a dozen roses," Papa said, smiling gently.
"Any other good news?"

"I got an A in my spelling test today," I said shyly.

"Excellent!" Papa cried. "Do you know the meanings
of the new words?"

I flushed, for I had merely memorized all the words,
sounding them out—*terrestrial, equatorial, longitude, lati-
tude.*

"No," I admitted.

Papa reached over to the niche in the wall. It contained
a dictionary, ragged and lop-eared. "Look them up," he
said. "When you learn the words, I want you to teach
the rest of us."

"I will, Papa," I said.

"We have to learn English," he continued. "From now on," he declared loudly, "no more German in the house. Only English."

We nodded meekly. Papa had made such edicts before. They were impossible to keep. German was our mother tongue. We could not change our identity so quickly. I wished we could have! Some people hated us because we were German; others because we were Jews. Like Mr. Hagen, Lester's father.

The Hagens lived on the second floor. Lester was a year older than I, very tall and skinny, with red hair like his father's. In every other way, though, he and his father were entirely different. I was terrified of Mr. Hagen, even before that dreadful afternoon.

That afternoon the weather was almost like spring, and a few leaves had started to sprout on the naked old trees stuck into the asphalt in front of our street.

Annie and I were skating on the sidewalk. I had gotten a pair of roller skates from the Goodwill store. They cost me forty cents. I loved to skate, and I was good at it, flying along the sidewalk, racing the cars. Mother said she used to skate like that when she was a young girl; she said I had good balance, because of the dancing lessons I'd taken in Germany.

But with Annie there, I had to share. We each wore one skate, trying tricks, linking arms and becoming "Siamese twins," each skating on one foot, the other foot raised.

Along came Lester Hagen on his two-wheeler. Lester had let me ride his bike a few times; I still wobbled, but I was determined to learn.

"Want to borrow my bike?" Lester asked amiably.

"Sure," I said.

Lester gave me the bike. "Want to borrow my skates?" I asked.

"Sure. What about Annie?"

"I will let her ride here," I said. "On the top."

"Handlebars," Lester said.

"Handlebars," I repeated, smiling.

"Better wait until you get the feel of it," Lester said.

"Okay," I said.

It was always easy to talk to Lester. He never asked me to repeat. He taught me new words without making me feel stupid.

Annie and I took off our skates and handed them to Lester. He sat down on the curb and, with the skate key, loosened them to make them longer for his feet.

After several false starts, I mounted the bike and began a wobbly ride down the street, with Annie running after. I could not turn, so I jumped off, turned the bike around, and headed back.

Then I saw Lester, still with the skates in his hands, his father bent over him, red faced and shouting.

"Oh, God," I murmured to Annie. Slowly we wheeled the bicycle back.

"And what in tarnation is that little kike doing with your bicycle? Hey? Answer me when I talk to you. Is that how you take care of the things I give you?"

A hard slap followed the question. Another slap, and Lester reeled back.

"I told you to stay away from them, didn't I? Didn't I? I'm going to give you such a lickin' you'll never forget."

"Pa! Pa!" Lester cried, trying to protect his eyes from his father's fist.

I saw a spurt of blood come from Lester's face. My hands were like ice, and I felt the icy ache pouring through my chest as I grabbed Annie and pulled her inside.

We ran up the stairs, flung ourselves into the house, and ran to our beds, panting.

Annie was screaming and crying. "Why did he do it? Lester is so nice. Why would he beat him like that? Why?"

That night Papa groaned when we told him. "God! That poor, poor boy. The man is a tyrant. Worse than an animal."

"But why did he get so angry about the bicycle?" Annie asked.

"It wasn't the bicycle, Annie," Mother said. "It was for playing with you."

"He's a member of the German-American Bund," Papa explained. "American friends of Hitler." His nostrils flared in anger. "They are the ones who held that big rally last month."

Rallies were commonplace in the city. KEEP US OUT OF WAR! said the placards, and speakers thundered in the square, "America first! We'll never again send American boys to fight in Europe. Let them fight their own bloody wars!"

I remembered Germany with its parades and speeches, Nazi parades. We'd been terrified of parades back then; we still were now.

"That's how it starts," Mother said in a low voice. "Parades and speeches first, then they start with the beatings, the arrests . . ."

"No, no," Papa said, waving his hand. "America is not Germany. Here everyone can speak freely. Even Nazis. But the difference is that here they must also follow the law."

"We once had laws in Germany, too," Mother argued.

"It is different here," Papa said firmly, and then, "Bed-time, girls." From our room we heard them talking. "Margo, we have to keep a good face in front of the children. We can't always be filling them with worries."

"I know, Arthur. I'm sorry. They already know too much."

"I've decided what to do with the money I earn Friday night. I'm going to surprise them. . . ."

Then there were whispers, nothing more, as I wrote in my diary:

March 3, 1941. Lester's father beat him badly this after-noon, just for playing with Annie and me. How could he do that to his own son? Lester's not supposed to play with us because we are Jews. Is something really wrong with Jews, that everybody hates us? Ruth says that some people are jealous, because they think all Jews are rich. Rich! That's a laugh.

I'm going to learn English so well that nobody will ever know I was German. I'm going to change. American girls are always running and laughing. I can do that, too!

Papa said he's bringing a surprise. I hope it's something I want. Often he brings things he thinks we want—it isn't the same at all. I know I'm supposed to love both my parents the same, but sometimes I love Papa more. I hate to say this, but I promised to be honest in my diary.

That Friday night, although I tried hard to stay awake, I fell asleep and was awakened by, of all things, singing!

"Oh, Columbia the jam of the ocean!"

Papa! He always sang about the "jam" of the ocean. We all rushed out.

There in the center of our tiny living room stood Papa with a large white pack slung over his back.

"What is it?" we cried. "What did you bring?"

"You will see." Slowly Papa lowered the white pack onto the card table, and now we saw that it was a large tablecloth, bundled up and tied at the corners.

"Sit down, everybody," Papa said grandly. He questioned us. "What did you have for dinner?"

Mama looked around, then said, "Soup. Bean and barley. And bread."

"No meat?" Papa asked.

"Arthur, you know that . . ."

"You had no meat at all?"

"Arthur, what is this questioning . . . ?"

But Mother was smiling slightly; she knew his tricks.

Grandly, ceremoniously, Papa reached out, slowly untied one corner, then the next, pulling back the cloth slowly, slowly, until all was revealed, and Papa's voice rang out. "Eat! Eat!"

We gazed at the bounty: Thick pieces of steak. Whole baked potatoes. White rolls. Olives and celery and plump, red radishes.

"They gave you food?" Mother gasped. "And ten dollars?"

"Leftovers," Papa said with a smile. "Those rich people don't eat much. They leave half of everything on the table."

We ate. And as we ate, Papa told us the story, until we rolled with laughter, of how the absent waiter's clothes had to be pinned onto him, for that man had the bulk of a giant, and our papa was but five-foot-seven, and thin.

"But it was wonderful," Papa said. "You cannot imagine, the table linen, flowers everywhere, candles . . ."

"Did you bring us any candles, Papa?" I asked.

"No." He shook his head. "What do you want with candles, child?"

I had always loved candles. Friday nights, we used to light them at home for the Sabbath. I was embarrassed to say anything.

We saved half the meat for tomorrow, but we ate everything else, and when we thought we were finished, Papa reached into his pocket and brought out twelve absolutely beautiful little cookies, only a little bit smashed.

"Papa," I sighed happily, "thank you."

"Wait until tomorrow!" he said.

The next day Papa went out to the secondhand store and returned with a bicycle. It was used and chipped; the rubber on the handlebars was cracked, but I thought it was magnificent.

"For the three of you to share," Papa said.

We were ecstatic.

"Is it safe, Arthur?" Mama asked anxiously, twisting her hands.

"Nothing is completely safe," Papa replied with a wink at me. "Sometimes we have to take our chances. Isn't that so, Monkey-face?"

I agreed.

Ruth didn't really care much about bike riding, and Annie fell heir to the skates. So, really, the bicycle was mine. I rode it every day after school unless it was raining or snowing. Sometimes Lester rode past on his bicycle, too. He never turned his face, never looked at me. I thought that in the set of his back I glimpsed his misery. I felt sorrier for Lester than anyone I knew.

Chapter 3

SOMEBODY HAD TO GO to school to see Annie's teacher. She had sent a note home.

"It's impossible!" Papa shouted. "How can we leave work to see your teacher? Annie, have you been naughty at school?"

Annie looked upset, pressing close to Mother.

Now Papa lowered his voice. "Annie, dear, there has to be a reason why the teacher needs to see us. What is it?"

"I need a white dress," Annie whispered miserably. "I told the teacher I didn't have one. She said to give you this note."

"Why do you need a white dress?" Papa demanded. "What kind of studies . . ."

"For the Easter program," said Annie, and burst into tears.

"Stop crying!" we all said. "What is it? What program?"

Haltingly, amid sobs, she told us. "I'm supposed to be

an angel. In the Easter play. I need a white dress. We all sing a song, but I—I have a speaking part, too.''

"If she doesn't have a white dress''—I then caught on—"she can't be in the play.''

"Why would a Jewish child be chosen for an Easter play?'' Mother cried. "I don't like it. I don't like it at all. Your grandfather would turn over in his grave.''

"They don't pay attention,'' Papa said. "Jewish, Christian—it's not *religious*. They just have a play.''

"You are telling me that Easter is not religious?'' Mother exclaimed, hands on her hips, and furious. "Don't you know what has happened, Easters past, when the gentiles accused us of using . . .''

"This is a play, Margo!'' Papa shouted. "The child only wants to be like all the other children in her class.''

"She's not like the other children!''

"Yes, she is!''

"Why does everybody always make such a big deal out of everything?'' Ruth wanted to know. She bit her lip. "So, it's a play about Christ. You can't expect them to do a play about Moses, when most of the kids are Christian.''

"It's America,'' Papa said, "not Palestine.''

"What are your lines, Annie?'' I asked. I hated to hear them fighting about this. I felt torn between them, Mama wanting things the way they were, Papa needing to be so American.

"I have only one line.'' Annie took a deep breath, put back her head and called out, " 'Praise be to God, he is risen!' ''

"Risen?'' I echoed. "You mean *raised.''*

"No! *Risen!''* Annie shouted.

"What does it mean, *risen*?'' Mama cried, distracted.

"Up, up!" Annie exclaimed. "Up from the dead. Jesus'
body floats up out of the grave. Goes to heaven. That's
the story," Annie said, looking well satisfied with herself.

In silence we looked at each other.

"Easter is a national holiday in the United States,
Margo," Papa said softly.

I could feel Mother weighing it.

"Let her do it, Mother!" we all cried.

"Quiet," Mother said sternly. "They talk about Christ
getting up from the dead—and Annie is supposed to play
this? How can she? What does she know about such things?"

"She doesn't have to know much, Mother," Ruth said.
"She only has to say . . ."—and Ruth began to giggle—
"Risen. Risen. Like bread dough!"

We collapsed in laughter, until we saw Mother's face.

"We came here because they wouldn't let us live,"
Mama said, her breathing heavy. "Now we are here, and
we live, but how?"

"I do my best, Margo," Papa said softly.

"You know I don't mean money, Arthur," Mother replied.

"We know what you mean, Margo," Papa said softly.
"But look, this is not a big thing. Annie will be in the
play, a beautiful angel. They chose her for her beauty, so
let them all see how beautiful our little girl is!"

"She still doesn't have a dress," I reminded them.

"All right." Papa threw up his hands, staring at Mother.
"If you say no, Margo, then it's no. But remember, we
have always taken other holidays, to enjoy them with our
friends. Don't you remember in Germany, the time we
hid the Easter eggs?"

"I remember," Mother said with a deep sigh. "I remember, too, we used to go to my parents' house for Passover.

Remember the Seder, all the people? All the cousins, aunts and uncles . . ."

"And your father read the Haggadah—how he went on! I thought those prayers would last the whole night, and we were famished."

"Mama cooked for five days, I remember. She washed every dish by hand, every piece of silver had to be polished. . . ."

Her voice faded. Mother and Father sat, both of them, silent now, transported.

In the past three years we'd slipped away from everything except Hannukah, which we celebrated modestly; Papa brought home candy, and Mother made cookies, with which she decorated our plates.

I wanted to say something. I wanted to call out, "Let's have a Seder here! Why don't we?" But I knew the answer by the tiredness in Mother's face. By the bend of Papa's back I saw his burdens, trying to make ends meet, then having to calculate the cost of a festival meal, candles, special matzos . . . it would not be a happy time, only a strain. They used that word lately—*strain*.

"What about Annie's dress?" I said.

Mother shook her head.

"Maybe I can get some white material," Papa said.

"I could help make it," I said quickly. I was taking a sewing class at school, and I loved using the machine. Ever since I was a little child I had made dolls' clothes by hand, using the bags of bright scraps Papa brought home from his shop.

Papa nodded. "I'll cut out the dress. We'll fit it on Annie together. You can stitch it at school. Then, I'll make the hem by hand. Very elegant." Papa brought his fingertips to his lips in an extravagant gesture. "Annie, you'll look like a queen."

"She's supposed to be an angel," Ruth said.

"We'll make her a halo," I added.

"Well, there are angels, too," Mother said through pursed lips, "in Jewish stories. Yes, I remember angels from my childhood. Lisa, you go to Annie's teacher tomorrow and tell her we are making a dress." Mother pulled herself up. "She shouldn't think we can't make a dress for our daughter."

The next day I stood before Annie's teacher at lunchtime.

"Your sister is a very good student," Miss Newcomb said. "She reads beautifully. Do you help her with her reading at home?"

"No, ma'am," I said.

Annie twisted her foot nervously.

"In fact, she is far above her grade level," the teacher continued. "That's why I wanted to talk to your parents."

What had this to do with Easter and a white dress? I was baffled. "My parents can't come," I said. "They work all the time."

"Then who takes care of you children?"

"I take care of Annie."

The teacher smiled slightly. "I see. Well, she's getting along just fine. Did she tell you we chose her to be an angel in the Easter play?"

"Yes, ma'am. And we're making her a white dress."

"That's lovely, dear. But it won't be necessary. You see, we are planning to make the costumes here, out of sheets."

I glared at Annie. She looked startled, then went blank, staring out the window.

"I wanted to talk to you about Annie's reading. She has taken to it like a duck to water."

I had no idea what the teacher was talking about. Ducks? Water? Annie?

"I'd like to skip her into second grade. If it's all right with your parents," Miss Newcomb said.

"*I see.*" I looked at Annie. She stood stock-still, her eyes round, enormous.

"Do you think your parents would approve? Is it all right? Yes?"

I took a deep breath. After all, I had been sent, I was to make the decision. "Yes," I said. "Let her go."

"Well, actually, she'll be in the same classroom. I teach both first and second graders in this room. But Annie will sit with the second graders, and it will go on her record. She will graduate from high school one year early, when she is seventeen, you see."

I nodded. Who cared when Annie would graduate from high school? All I could think about was the honor, the honor to Annie and therefore to all of us, having a child who was so smart.

On the way home I wanted to grab Annie, give her hugs. I kept myself back. Instead, I scolded her for not understanding about the white dress. "You have to listen better," I said.

"I'm the best reader in the whole class," she said.

"Don't be so conceited," I said.

"Now maybe Mother will let me have the cat."

"You're dreaming," I said.

Just the day before Annie had spotted a cat lurking around the coal chute. It was a dingy gray, with green-yellow eyes and black spots on its face, quite the ugliest cat I had ever seen, not nearly as pretty as the cat we had left behind in Germany.

"Oh, how beautiful!" cried Annie. She bent down. Instantly the cat nuzzled Annie's face. She cradled it against her chest, swaying with it, crooning, "Oh, oh, my beautiful cat, I'll call you Hansi. Sweet, sweet Hansi."

"Mother will never let you keep it upstairs," I said.

"Why not?" Annie asked, all innocence.

"She'll say the cat is dirty. It's a stray." I remembered my beautiful, elegant Siamese.

"So what? You don't know! Mama will love it. She loves to take care of little animals. You'll see."

When we arrived home Annie told me, "I'm going to take Hansi upstairs."

"You'll be sorry!" I warned.

But Annie wouldn't listen. Mother and Father were at their class that night. Annie left a note: "Dear Mama, I love you so much. Teacher says I am so smart I can go to second grade. Thank you for letting us keep the kitty. She was an orphan."

When Mother and Papa came in to check on us, Annie was sound asleep. I kept my eyes closed, pretending.

I felt them gazing at us.

The cat was curled against Annie's chest.

"That child is really smart," Papa whispered. "She takes after my mother."

"Thank you very much!" Mama exclaimed. "Where does she get these words? An orphan."

"I hope it's a good mouser," Papa said.

"That's the ugliest creature I've ever seen," Mother whispered. "But . . . the child has suffered enough. She deserves something of her own."

A week or so later when Ruth found the cat on her bed, lying on top of her skirt, she was furious.

"Get that disgusting animal out of here!" Ruth cried.

"Leave Hansi alone," Annie screamed.

"I don't want him in my room! He has fleas and dirt."

"It's my room, too."

"If you don't keep that cat off my bed, I'll toss him out the window."

The battle was on. Annie shrieked, lunged at Ruth, who slapped back, while Annie kicked, then ran. Ruth tore after her, shouting threats. Annie dashed into the little hallway, out the glass door, slamming it back behind her, and in the next instant I heard, mingled with their shouts, a terrible splintering crash.

Everything stopped. Glass sprinkled down from the hole in the pane, and as I looked, I became aware of the blood spurting from a gash in Ruth's arm.

Ruth stood there wavering, as if she would drop.

Somehow I remembered instructions, burned into my mind from a lesson in first aid. I ran to get a towel, and with it I bound Ruth's arm.

"Lisa! Lisa!" Ruth moaned over and over again, her lips pale with shock.

"Come on," I cried, taking her other arm. "Hurry." I led her downstairs the four flights, biting my lips to keep from screaming, at last reaching the Morellis' door.

I pounded on the door.

No response.

I pounded again, calling, "Mrs. Morelli! Mrs. Morelli!"

Then I remembered. It was Wednesday. Her children went to catechism on Wednesdays.

Someone shouted angrily, "Quiet out there! I'm sleeping!

What the devil do you think this is—a man has to get some rest!''

Mr. Granowski worked nights; he would never come out to help us.

In the hall I saw the gaping hole where once a pay telephone had been. For some reason it was gone now, and even if it had been there, I would not have known whom to call.

Ruth was slumped on the stair, her face an ashen white as blood seeped into the towel, leaving deep red stains. "Lisa," she whispered. "Lisa."

"Wait here!" I shouted. "Annie—stay with her."

A blustery wind blew my skirt up around my legs as I ran the two blocks to the little corner grocery store, where four or five people waited in line.

I pushed past them. One woman raised her hand warningly. "Get in line," she cried.

"Wait your turn, girlie," said a man.

"My sister is hurt. We need a doctor. Now!"

The storekeeper looked up. He shook his head, perplexed.

I realized then, to my horror, that I had spoken in German.

The woman in line stared at me. "I'm in a hurry," she said.

Mutely I stood there, never before so helpless. I ran back to the apartment, fighting against the wind, pushing at the heavy door with all my might. Ruth was half lying across the step with her head in Annie's lap. I ran up the first flight of stairs and pounded on Lester Hagen's door.

For an instant I imagined Mr. Hagen's face, his beefy arms, and I shuddered.

The door swung open.

Lester stood there. "It's Ruth!" I cried. "She's hurt. Help me. Hurry! Please!" I was sobbing.

Lester rushed down, took one look, and lifted Ruth in his arms. "Open the door!" he told me.

"Where are you taking her?" I cried.

"Do it!" he shouted.

We ran behind Lester as he made his way through the busy, freezing streets to the basement entrance of a small, dingy clinic with barred windows and delapidated chairs, where several people waited for help.

"Emergency," Lester panted, still holding Ruth, who leaned her head against him.

In a moment she was taken inside; I went with her. Lester and Annie waited with the others.

The doctor, a young man, shook his head, bit his lip, while first he gave Ruth an injection, then carefully worked to remove the splinters of glass.

"Don't look," he told me.

I did not obey. I stood gazing at his deft fingers, the set of his mouth, the way he worked. I became horribly aware of my mussed hair, my limp dress, my freckles.

The doctor glanced at me. "You're pretty spunky, aren't you?"

I said nothing; I did not know the word. I felt that I was barely breathing, first from the shock of seeing Ruth hurt, then from the greater shock of standing beside this young doctor, who was so handsome that it hurt me to look at him.

The doctor put twenty stitches in the gash on Ruth's arm. Then he told her to lie down for a few minutes, while he gave her juice to drink and cookies to eat.

He offered me a cookie, too. I had no appetite.

Out in the waiting room Annie and Lester jumped up.

"She'll be all right," the doctor said. "She can go home in a few minutes." The doctor peered at Annie's neck. "How long has she had that rash?" he asked.

"What rash?" I went to look. There was a round spot, reddish brown, like layered rings on the side of her neck.

"Does it itch?" the doctor asked.

Annie nodded.

He drew her under the light. "Looks like ringworm," he said.

"What's that?" I asked.

"A skin disease," he said. "Very contagious."

"Contagious?" I asked.

"If you were close to her," he said, "you will get it, too."

"We sleep in the same bed," I told him.

"Yup," he said cheerfully, "you'll get it for sure."

"What does it come from?" I asked.

"Often from stray cats," he said. "I have good news for you," he continued.

"What?" I breathed. In my imagination he was inviting me to a ball, like Cinderella, not in a coach, but in a beautiful Chevrolet.

"If you catch it, you'll be out of school for two weeks, maybe three."

"That's not good news," I told him. "I like school."

He looked surprised, then smiled and told me, "I guess foreign kids are more serious students."

When we got back to the apartment, Mother and Father were already home, and frantic.

"We saw the broken glass! The blood!"

"We're all right," I said, and explained it all. "We took care of everything. Lester helped us."

"A prince," said Papa.

He threw the cat out that very night, even while Annie sobbed and screamed. "We cannot keep an animal that will make us sick," Papa said firmly.

In my diary I wrote,

May 28, 1941. What's the matter with me? All I can think about is going back to see that doctor again. Of course, he only thinks of me as a "foreigner." Sometimes I wish there was no such thing as different countries. Then people would all be the same. Those people in the store probably thought I was stupid, because I was babbling in German. They looked at me the way they look at that retarded man who hangs around the newsstand on the corner.

I thought Ruth was going to die today. When she got so white, I was scared. If Ruth died, it would have been my fault. Sometimes I cannot understand myself. Even when Ruth was so hurt, I was thinking how handsome the doctor was. I must have an evil streak in me. Like those monsters in the movies. I wonder where it came from?

Chapter 4

THAT SUMMER a wonderful thing happened. A class in gymnastics and dance was offered at the YWCA. I had never heard of this organization before, and I was amazed that they gave classes for anybody who wanted to go, for only fifty cents. Papa gave me the money when I wasn't able to earn it by baby-sitting.

It was the first dance class I'd had in three years. We did not do ballet, but tap and modern dance. The teacher found an old pair of tap shoes for me; I was in heaven. The class continued that fall and into winter. I made friends there, too. So, when Papa started talking about leaving New York, I had mixed feelings.

One night, when Papa came home late from working at a banquet, I got up to see him. We stood at the kitchen counter together, sipping hot tea with plenty of sugar and milk in it. I saw how Papa's hand shook when he picked up the cup. I thought of all the extra things he bought for us, and how hard he had worked to get them—a used sofa, a real table, a secondhand radio. More than anything, I wanted to make him proud of me.

"Papa, I'm going to be a great dancer some day," I said. "Wait and see. The teacher at the Y says I'm one of the best in the class."

"You should have ballet lessons," Papa said. "From a fine teacher." He sighed. "I'm thinking of doing a little extra business," Papa said. "I can get a bargain on a case of glass ashtrays from a man going out of business. He made a lot of money on novelties." Papa reached into his pocket and took out an old envelope, made calculations. "After I have paid everything, I figure, I can make ten cents profit apiece."

"How?"

"The ashtrays are in the shape of stars. There's a place in the middle for a candle. I figured, I'll get some gold felt, cut out stars, and glue them onto the bottom of the ashtrays, to make them pretty, and not to scratch the table. What do you think?"

"I don't know, Papa. Do you think people will want to buy them?"

"Your mother says no."

"How many ashtrays are there?"

"Five hundred."

"That's fifty dollars!" I exclaimed.

"With fifty dollars," Papa said, "I could probably get two bus tickets to California."

"California!" I exclaimed. I remembered the orange crates.

"Shh . . . don't wake the others. Don't mention anything," he hastily added. "Maybe I'm just dreaming . . . but listen. I have a feeling about California. Do you know they never have winter there? Sunshine every day. Not so crowded—a man can make a good living there. Everything in New York is too expensive.''

"I'd love to go to California, Papa," I whispered. "But what about my class at the Y?''

Papa's brows shot up in amazement. "What's the matter with you? Don't you know that the best dancers and the best teachers are in Hollywood, California? The way to get famous is to go to California!''

That Sunday morning, right after breakfast, Papa turned our little living room into a workshop.

"Ruth! Come, enough chemistry already—we'll all work together. Margo! Come, make us a pattern. Annie, you can gather up the scraps. And find something nice for us on the radio.''

We worked for about an hour. My nose itched from the felt; glue stuck to my fingers. Ruth and I had planned to go to the movies that afternoon to see a musical, *Babes on Broadway*. I had saved enough money to treat Ruth; she didn't usually baby-sit, because she was busy studying hard subjects like botany and math.

I kept looking at the clock, realizing we couldn't make the first show, calculating when the next show would start. I didn't dare complain. After all, these glass ashtrays were our ticket to a new world!

We stopped to count.

"Thirty-eight!" Papa exclaimed.

"Only four hundred sixty-two to go," Ruth said dryly. Cartons of glass ashtrays stood stacked against the walls. Five hundred of anything, I realized, is a *lot*.

"What if nobody wants these, Papa?" Ruth asked. "We might be doing all this work for nothing.''

"I'm bored," Annie said. "I want to go outside.''

"What a bunch of complainers!" Papa exclaimed.
"Where's your spirit?"

"They are children," Mother said gently.

"I was only fourteen years old," Papa declared, "when
I was sent to live in town with a tailor, as his apprentice.
Do you know how many hours I worked every day? Fourteen
hours. From six in the morning until eight at night."

Papa had told me the story before, how homesick he
was, so that he cried in his bed at night, and how on
Sundays he walked all the way home to see his mother
for just an hour before he had to set off back again.

"Well, I expected this, and I am prepared," Papa said
with a flourish. "Just a moment."

He disappeared into the bedroom and returned with a
white sack, placing it in the middle of the table.

"Close your eyes and feel."

We did.

"Now taste!"

We tasted. Annie grinned.

"Popcorn," Papa said. "Very American food. Now we
eat for five minutes, then work some more."

A sudden, harsh interruption changed everything. Soft
music from the radio was cut off abruptly by a man's voice.
"Ladies and gentlemen, this is a special news bulletin.
We now have confirmed reports that enemy planes have
bombed American bases in Honolulu."

Annie went on sorting through the gold stars. The rest
of us froze.

". . . Early this morning Japanese planes attacked
American ships anchored at Pearl Harbor in the Hawaiian
Islands, inflicting severe damage. Casualties are now esti-
mated at . . ."

"Where are the Hawaiian Islands?" Ruth whispered.

"Enemy planes . . ." I gasped.

"But . . . but Hawaii," Mother stammered. "Isn't that on the other side of the world?"

"Hush." Papa raised his hand to silence us as he bent near to the radio, his features compressed into a deep, granite frown.

Still, the announcer's sharp voice hammered out words I could hardly grasp. ". . . the predawn surprise attack . . . tons of TNT . . . United States ships crippled in the harbor . . . confusion, panic, loss of life . . ."

Papa turned for a moment from the radio and said, "It means war. For us. World war."

A chill rushed down my spine. War. I knew about that. I had seen the beginnings of war in Germany, gangs of toughs beating old Jews on the streets, windows being smashed, people being searched, arrested, thrown into prison, their houses destroyed.

"But why?" Mother whispered. "How could it be? You said the American people didn't want to go to war, even to help England."

"The Japanese attacked Hawaii," Papa explained. "Hawaii belongs to the United States. Don't you understand? They attacked *us*."

"*Us?*" I exclaimed. "What do you mean, Papa?"

"*Us*," he cried, standing up now, and straining. "It was an act of war for Japanese planes to bomb our territory. We will be at war now with Japan, and Japan is an ally of the Germans, so we must fight Germany on one side of the world and Japan on the other . . . oh, God! God help us!"

We sat there, dazed. The doorbell rang. Papa went to answer. It was Mrs. Morgenstrom.

"You have heard the news?" she said, her arms extended.

"Oh, my dears," she said, and she burst into tears.

"Girls, clear away those things," Mother said in a strange voice.

We pushed ashtrays, stars, and scraps into boxes.

As we followed Mama into the kitchen, Annie whispered to me, "Why is Mama upset?"

I shook my head and sighed. "We're at war," I said.

In the kitchen Mother's hands fluttered over her tasks. "Papa brought home some rolls last night," she said. "Put them on a plate. Bring out some jam. I will make a few hard-boiled eggs and tea."

"Mama—why do we have to do all this?"

"Because we have a guest in our house, that's why!" Mama said fiercely. "Now, go put this cloth on the table. Take in the sugar bowl. Annie, pick up those crayons right now!"

Somehow the day passed. Mrs. Morgenstrom stayed awhile, her bursting talk filling our senses, until at last her tears silenced her and she left with the words, "What's to become of the world now? Oh, my dears, we thought the madness was over, and now it's just beginning!"

Neighbors opened their doors and came out into the halls. We looked into the faces of neighbors we had never really seen before. Mr. Granowski, his stiff, dark hairs standing up like a prickly crown, groaned as he confronted my father in the hall. "It means we'll all have to go. Young and old. They'll take us all into the army, wait and see."

We kept the radio on all day, and we listened to the same report over and over again, as late afternoon shadows appeared at the windows like ghosts.

Suddenly Mother asked, "Weren't you girls going to go to the movies?"

Ruth and I stared at each other. "Yes, but . . ."

"Go," Mama said. She went to the kitchen canister, where she kept some coins. "Go to the movies. Annie can go, too."

I was aghast. Mother always made us spend our own money for movies.

"Go and have a good time," she said. "Take ten cents extra for candy. Papa and I will walk over and pick you up when the show is over. It will already be dark."

Off we went, bundled up, first to select a dime's worth of assorted candies at the grocery store—a whole bag full.

The streets were the same as always, with clusters of people in front of theaters, some gathered around the news-stands, a few young lovers together kissing, some parents with baby carriages.

I remembered how it was that last morning when we left Berlin, seeing those streets, knowing I'd never go back again.

"It all looks normal," I murmured to Ruth, "but it isn't."

"Nothing ever is," Ruth replied.

Annie hopped along, pulling on my arm, singing:

"My mom gave me a nickel
To buy a pickle;
I didn't buy a pickle
I bought some chewing gum!
Choo-choo-choo-choo-choo chewing gum . . ."

We sat in the back row of the theater. Some boys came and tried to bother Ruth. She got rid of them, threatening to call the usher.

The movie was so beautiful, full of life. Judy Garland
sang like an angel, and everyone danced. The girls' skirts
whirled around their legs, and I could see their eyes shining,
and I knew how they felt to be dancing. Dancing! And
for the first time it occurred to me that the best life of all
would be to dance like that and actually get paid for it. I
had danced ever since I was seven years old and never
realized that, for some people, dancing was a profession.

Now I imagined myself in every role, as I sat in that
dark theater, part of me watching, the other part pretending.

Three times Annie had to be taken to the toilet. Each
time, I had to go with her. Ruth refused.

I knew better than to try to rush Annie. So I stood at
the bathroom mirror gazing at myself, trying to pout the
way Judy Garland did, using my arms as she did, feeling
beautiful.

When Mother and Papa met us, Ruth and Annie told
them all about the movie. I remained silent, saturated with
visions.

Mother and Father said nothing about the news or the
war. It was as if they had made a pact to ignore it, at
least for tonight.

At home our beds were cold. The super had forgotten
to stoke the furnace, I guess, in his preoccupation with
the news.

I wrote a single word in my diary that night: *"December
7, 1941. WAR!"*

The next morning President Roosevelt spoke on the radio:
"Yesterday, December 7, 1941, a date which will live in
infamy, the United States was attacked by naval and air
forces of the empire of Japan."

Pointing, Papa handed me the dictionary. I looked up
infamy, "evil reputation, outrageous act."

"Very many American lives have been lost," the president continued. "I have asked Congress to declare war on the empire of Japan. . . ."

Far into the night, we all lay on Mother and Father's bed, listening to the radio. Then, already half-asleep we went to our own beds, still hearing repetitions of the terrible news.

Just a few weeks later, I met Lester on the street. I'd been sent to the grocers for some potatoes. For once, Annie was not with me.

"Lisa!" He called me from across the street, and I waited up for him.

"I've been hoping I'd see you," Lester said. "How is Ruth's arm?"

"Just about healed," I said. "But she'll always have a scar."

"That's too bad," Lester said.

"Nobody will notice," I said. "She is so pretty." I blushed. I didn't know why I'd said that.

"I wanted to tell you that I'm leaving," Lester said. We both stopped walking.

"Where are you going?"

He frowned, turned slightly away, his hands in his pockets. "I enlisted in the navy," he said. "I don't know where they'll send me."

"You—enlisted? How could you? Are you old enough?"

Lester smiled. "Not quite. But they don't know that."

"You—you lied to the navy?"

"Just a little. I told them I'm seventeen. Lucky, I'm tall for my age."

I looked up at Lester. Yes, he was tall, and earnest, and very nice. I swallowed hard. I'd miss him, even though we really didn't see each other much.

"Why do you want to go?" I whispered.

"I'm sick of school," Lester said vehemently. "I've got to get out of here. There's a war going on! I want to be there, do something about it."

"But what about your father? Is he letting you go?"

Lester shook his head. "My father doesn't know anything about this."

"You didn't even tell him?"

"I'm leaving early Saturday morning. By the time he finds out, it'll be too late. He won't be able to stop me."

"But what about your mom?" I had seen Lester's mother, a plain woman, usually wearing an apron, carrying bundles up to her place. She never spoke, never smiled.

Lester took a deep breath. "It'll be better for them without me. The navy pays well. They won't have to bother about me anymore."

I smiled. "I wish I could see you in your sailor suit," I said.

"Maybe I'll write to you," he said.

"Oh, I think we won't be here."

"How come?"

"We might move to California. Don't tell anyone . . . It's not . . . ."

"It's not official," Lester said, nodding. "I won't say a word. Don't you, either."

"Of course not," I said.

"Well." Lester took my hand, clasped it briefly, hard. "See you," he said.

"See you," I replied.

I didn't think I would ever see Lester Hagen again.

Chapter 5

SINCE THAT NIGHT Papa had confided in me, we shared a secret. Although he had mentioned California to Mama, only I knew he was actually saving up money to go there. It was the only bright spot in those bleak days of the new year, 1942.

We were at war. Everything changed. People hurried more, worried more, changed jobs so they could help with the "war effort." We got used to seeing boys in uniform, and seeing newsreels about men fighting from tanks and ships and planes.

Somehow the world had turned gray. Lights were dim in the streets; no light could show from the air, since enemy planes might come overhead, loaded with bombs.

At school the teachers told us what to do in case of an air attack. Drills were held every week. No matter what the weather, we stood out in the yard, watching the gray skies for signs of enemy planes. In case of a real attack, we were supposed to hurry home. They said that the warning system would give us fifteen or twenty minutes to get off the streets. In terror we rehearsed it.

Those of us who had younger sisters or brothers at the elementary school were told where to meet up with them. I'd meet Annie on the corner, grab her arm, and run back to the apartment, dodging traffic, my heart beating like a drum.

"Slow down! Stop! It's just a drill," Annie would pant.

Still I pulled her onward; I was never sure. If enemy planes did come, what would I do?

We were told at school, "Go to the nearest air-raid shelter." But there weren't enough air-raid shelters built. We also got alternate instructions: "Hide in a cellar. Stay away from windows. Avoid shattering glass. Keep calm!"

That was a laugh. I could not imagine anybody keeping calm while they were being killed.

Posters appeared in shop windows—UNCLE SAM WANTS YOU!—urging people to enlist.

Another poster showed a cocker spaniel grieving, its head on a discarded uniform. HE DIED BECAUSE SOMEONE TALKED. Anyone could be a spy. Boys in uniform didn't even tell their folks where they were being sent. The rest of us were warned: Keep silent. Don't talk to strangers; you might not even realize that information you have could be valuable to the enemy. We were very careful.

In another way, though, people were friendlier. Waiting in line or on the bus, strangers talked together about the latest shortages of rubber or sugar, gasoline, or meat.

Canned fruits and candy, jam, and cake began to disappear from store shelves. Sugar was being sent overseas. We complained about not having candy and gum; our parents told us that in Europe children were starving.

In our building some women started making money for the first time in their lives, working in factories. The first time Ruth and I saw a woman wearing pants, we were horrified. We were riding a bus and saw a group of the women walking together, swinging their arms, wearing overalls and caps.

I nudged Ruth. "Did you see that?"

"Disgusting," Ruth whispered. "Her bottom sticks out—I'd be so embarrassed."

"Why are they wearing pants?"

"They're war workers, honey," said the woman next to us. She smiled at me. "Soon you'll be seeing 'em all over. My sister works in a defense plant. My daughter's doing riveting, making tanks. She even uses a blowtorch!"

Soon even glamorous models in magazines were pictured in trousers!

"Well, well," Papa mused, "the world is not the same place anymore at all, with women wearing pants."

"I think they look fabulous," I said.

Mother pointed at me sternly. "Forget about it," she said. "You wear dresses and skirts, like a lady. Just because there's a war on, I will not have my girls running around like tramps."

"Marlene Dietrich, Betty Grable, June Haver—are they all tramps?" I argued. "They are wearing these darling little short pants, playsuits. . . ."

"Movie stars," Mother said scornfully. "Don't tell me what those women are doing. What has that to do with decent people?"

We saw different kinds of people on the streets, men in uniform, men carrying knapsacks on their backs, who obviously had never been to the big city before. They stood

staring up at the tall buildings, looking confused. Some
had gray hair, like Papa.

Annie asked Papa, "Will you be a soldier, too?"

"They don't want me," Papa said, rolling a cigarette.
"I'm too old." He tapped the ends of the cigarette, closing
one eye as he held the match near his face to light it. He
inhaled deeply.

"They would want you," I argued. "You'd be a wonderful soldier. Or you could design uniforms for the soldiers."

Papa said, "I was in World War One."

"You were?" We had never discussed this before, and
I was amazed.

"I was even decorated," Papa said. "Someday I'll show
you my medals."

"Not now, Arthur," Mother said in a low voice.
"They're put away. German medals . . ."

"You fought for the Germans?" I exclaimed.

"Of course. I was a German." He nodded slowly. "You
see how things change."

"Yes, now we are enemy aliens," Mother said. "They
don't trust us. Because we're German." She seemed upset.

"Well, they have to be careful," Papa soothed. "Some
Germans here in America want to sabotage the war. They'd
follow Hitler if they could."

"Not Jews!" Mother cried. "We're certainly loyal to
the United States."

"They don't know who is and who isn't," Papa pointed
out, "so we all have to register and keep the curfew. It's
not so terrible, being in by ten-thirty at night. Time for
working people to be in bed anyhow."

"It's the principle of the thing," Mother exclaimed.
"That's how it started in Germany. Jews having to register."

"It's not because we're Jews!" Papa cried. "Margo,

you'll make yourself crazy with this kind of thinking. Nobody is persecuting us here. They want to keep track of us because we are still foreigners. Once we get our citizenship papers . . ."

"That takes five years!" Mother broke in.

"Then we'll be like everyone else. Citizens. Miss Tatcher told us, didn't you listen? We'll be like everyone else, except we can't run for president. So, who wants to be president anyhow? Maybe you, but not me." He laughed, slapping his thigh. "That would be something, wouldn't it? A Jew for president? Well, this is America. Anything can happen."

Mother shook her head. "It would never happen. Look, I want you girls to be careful. Out on the street, don't talk German. Don't attract attention. You never know. If there is trouble, they might send us back."

"Margo," Papa began, "please don't . . ."

"I'll never go back there!" Annie cried. "Never! I hate everything German."

"You can't hate everything," Ruth pointed out. "We're German."

"Margo, don't paint everything so black. See now, you've upset the little one."

"Listen, I hear people in the restaurant," Mother said, breathing fast, her eyes darting about. "Politics, war, that's all they talk about. And it goes against the Japanese, against the Germans, against everyone who isn't American by birth. I don't even open my mouth. If they hear my accent, right away they are suspicious. So I keep quiet. All day, quiet. Maybe they think I am a spy."

Papa and I burst out laughing. Mama, a spy! Mama laughed, too. It was good to hear her laugh.

"So now at home," Papa said, smoking and smiling,

"you talk politics. Never before, Margo, did you talk politics."

"When did I have time for politics in Germany?" Mother chuckled. "I was far too busy going to cafés and the theater, and planning parties. Remember the parties we used to have, Arthur? Remember the opera?" She smiled at Papa. "Ah, we had some wonderful times, my dear."

I loved it when she called him "my dear." So often lately, instead of tenderness between them, there were arguments. As the days went on, they argued more and more about California. Ruth, Annie, and I heard them from our room at night.

"I'm used to New York," Mother said. "I like it here."

"You haven't seen any other parts of the country!" Papa exclaimed. "How can you know what you like best?"

"I know I'm satisfied," Mother retorted. "Why look for trouble?"

"My friends tell me it's better out West," Papa said. "Life is easier. The truth is, Margo, there's nothing for me here. You were right. Nobody wanted the ashtrays. I can't even give them away."

"So you want to spend our last few dollars moving us to California?" Mother cried.

"Better to move now than to wait until all the money's gone. Then we won't have a choice."

"And what about my mother?" Mama cried.

"What?" Papa exclaimed. "What has your mother to do with this?"

"How will the authorities ever know where to find us if we move? It's been so long, and no word from Mother at all. How can I even notify her of our new address if we move?"

"We'll just write to the consul in Germany. Give him our new address. Then when it is time for your mother to get her visa . . ."

"No. They will not give her a visa," Mother said.

"What are you talking about?"

"The letter from the authorities came yesterday."

"Margo, why didn't you tell me?"

Silence. Then Mother's voice came, muffled. "They have a long waiting list . . . Arthur, Mama can't wait! The situation over there gets worse every day. They are even putting old people in concentration camps; you know it!"

"Margo, she will keep out of their way somehow. The war won't last forever. When it is over, I promise you, I'll go there and get her myself and bring her to you. Margo, I *promise*!"

"What do you think happened to Grandmother?" I whispered to Ruth. "Mama writes to her, but she never gets an answer."

"She probably . . ." Ruth sighed. "I don't know. People don't just disappear."

"They have been arresting Jews," I said. "More and more. Even women. Even little children." We heard horrible stories. At night, when the adults were talking, or on an occasional Sunday afternoon when there were guests, they spoke about it, their voices hard and hushed, talking about torture, arrests, concentration camps, and killings. Mass killings in unimaginably brutal ways.

"How can this go on?" The adults groaned, incredulous. "How can the world just sit by and do nothing?"

"Some people don't know," they said. "Or they don't want to know. I read a book about concentration camps . . . Hitler's plan. He calls it the 'final solution.' "

"Final solution?"

"Yes. He plans to exterminate . . . ."

"Hush now, hush." Someone always ended it. "Enough talk!"

Now Ruth said, "Maybe Grandma went to another country. Some people are going to China."

I almost laughed in spite of myself. "Our grandmother? In China? She'd never do that."

"I guess you're right," Ruth said. "Grandma would never change her life that way."

"I would," I said staunchly. "I'd love to go to China. I'd love to travel and see the whole world."

"Not me."

"Don't you even want to go to California?"

"No."

"Why not?"

Irritably, Ruth shoved her books aside, got up, and began to pace. "It's just like you to want to rush off the minute we get settled somewhere. You can't stick to anything. No wonder you get such lousy grades in school."

"I don't get lousy grades!" I did, of course, compared to Ruth.

"Mother's right. Why look for change? Things could be worse."

"Or they could be better," I cried. "Don't you ever get tired of the same thing day after day? Don't you want to see something new?"

"I'm tired of being dragged all over the world!" Ruth exclaimed. "I want to settle down, be sure of the next day, be able to find my way when I go places. I hate getting lost, having to ask directions, never really belonging anywhere, not having friends. . . ."

"Ruth, you've got me."

She shrugged. "It doesn't matter what we want, anyhow. Papa will decide, like he always does. And that means we'll go. You know how he is."

Ruth settled herself down on her bed. "At least schools are easier in California. That's what I've heard."

"Why would that be?" I asked.

"Everyone goes to the beach and lies in the sun all the time."

"It sounds like heaven," I sighed.

"If you want to be a lazy animal," Ruth retorted.

"What's wrong with having a little fun?" I objected.

"A little is all right," Ruth admitted, smiling. She jumped up. "Let's do our hair in pin curls," she suggested.

"Do you have enough bobby pins?"

"Yes. A whole pile."

Those, too, were hard to get, because of the rubber tips. Rubber was needed for the war effort.

"I'll do you first," Ruth said.

I sat down on the bed and Ruth knelt above me. She divided my hair into sections, made the twisted flat curls, pinning each one with two pins. "I missed too much school," she said under her breath.

"What do you mean?"

"In Switzerland. And when we were traveling. I didn't learn anything. We moved around so much. Now I'm way behind."

"How can you say you're behind? You're always studying."

"That's why."

"But you get terrific grades!" I turned to look at Ruth, saw the dark smudges under her eyes. She did get good grades, but the cost was high.

"I've got to get ready for entrance exams. Lisa, I want

to go to college. I want to make something of myself. I can't stand to live like this always, three of us in this little room, never knowing what's coming up next.''

"College? How could you? Isn't it terribly expensive?" I stared up at Ruth. Her face was flushed, and she bit her lip.

"I'm going to start saving," she said. "Also, I'm thinking, if I join the Women's Army Corps, maybe I can get my education free.''

"Be in the army?" I exclaimed. "But—wouldn't it be terribly dangerous? And you say you hate to travel.''

"I do," she admitted. "But on the other hand, I'd get to wear that uniform and that terrific hat. . . .''

We both laughed.

"Papa would never let you go," I said.

"Don't be so sure," Ruth said.

"I'd miss you!''

"Whatsa matter, girlie," Ruth said in a tough-gangster voice, "doncha know there's a war on?''

I fixed Ruth's hair in pin curls, and when I settled down to sleep, she was still sitting up reading. I had gotten used to hearing the pages turn while I slept.

College. I had never known anybody who went to college. I hadn't the least idea what went on there, except that when they came out, people were important. They earned a lot of money.

But to go to college, first of all you had to have money, and you had to be brilliant.

I'd never make it. Of course, a dancer doesn't have to go to college.

The classes at the Y had ended abruptly. The room was being used for army recruiting. I tried to practice on my own, using the kitchen counter to balance myself. I practiced pliés and tried to keep limber by stretching. But I knew very well that a dancer has to dance, and to take lessons continually in order to improve.

Unable to sleep, I got up to write in my diary.

January 12, 1942. I hope and pray we can go to California. Papa said there are thousands of fine dancing teachers there. Maybe the kids there will be nicer. I can start all over and make friends. Nobody needs to know where I came from.

Mama thinks we should stay in New York, and so does Ruth. Mama says California is too close to Japan, and we could get killed in an air raid! Our teacher says that Japan is in the war to get more land. She says that is what wars are always about. I think everything should be divided up equally. Rich people should give some of their money to the poor. It is the same with land.

Mother cannot find out where Grandmother is. Papa says maybe she has gone underground. Hiding. I wish we had been born here in America. Some kids at school don't know a thing about the war, and they don't even care. All they care about is how they look, and what clothes they can get.

Ruth started shaving her legs. I took Papa's razor and shaved mine, too. I think nice legs are really important, especially for a dancer. Boys like girls with nice legs. When the war is over, we'll be able to buy all the silk stockings we want. I'm so sick of the war!

In the end, of course, Papa got his way. He told Mother just to try it. If she didn't like California, we'd come back to New York.

I knew we never would. California, I thought, must be as close to heaven as anyone can get down here.

Chapter 6

MOTHER TOLD ME, "I want you girls to help me go through our things."

"What things?"

"Old clothes, shoes, extra canned goods. Before we leave," Mama said, "I am sending a box to Germany. To Clara."

"Clara!" With that name, a thousand memories rushed back at me, and I felt caught in a cyclone of emotions. Clara had taken care of me since I was born. When we left Germany, of course, we had to leave Clara behind, too.

"I have written to Clara asking her to try to find my mother." Busily Mother packed a large carton with powdered milk, cookies, canned tuna, pudding mix, noodle soup. Into a metal canister Mother carefully poured three pounds of flour.

It brought back memories. I used to help Clara in the kitchen, especially on Friday afternoons when we baked the braided bread called *challah* for the Sabbath meal. Those were happy times, with Annie in her high chair, Mother making soup and supervising the baking. We brushed the top of the risen bread with egg white, so that later it glistened by the light of our Sabbath candles.

I wondered, did Clara still bake bread in Berlin? Did she miss us?

Mother went around our house selecting things. "Might as well send this sweater, too. It's hot in California. I won't need it. When Clara finds my mother, she will share these things with her."

Suddenly Mother bent against the sink, her head down, her body heaving with sobs.

"Mama! Mama!" I ran to her. I put my arms around her.

"I should have made her come with us!" Mother said fiercely. "I should have forced her."

"You know you could never force Grandmother to do anything," I said. "She's so tough."

"Lisa, Lisa," my mother moaned. "What can I do? I pray to God every night for my mother, every night and every morning. I beg Him to watch over her. How could I bear it if anything happened, knowing that I did not save her?"

"But you tried, Mama!" I cried.

"If God saves her, I'll never complain about anything again. I swear it!" my mother declared. I had never seen her so panicked, even when we were leaving Germany and in great danger.

"I'll pray for her, too, Mama," I said earnestly. "She'll be all right, Mother," I soothed. "Wait and see. Grandmother will be fine."

"But every mile that we go closer to California," my

mother said, "takes me farther away from Germany, farther away from her."

We took the Greyhound bus to California. Annie was sick to her stomach almost the whole time. Twice she threw up. I was sitting right beside her.

The trip took five whole days. We occupied ourselves by telling stories or reading or watching the world on the other side of the highway. At nearly each stop a few servicemen got on or off, carrying duffel bags over their shoulders, saying good-bye to mothers and sweethearts. It made me think of Lester Hagen. I wondered where he was.

On the fifth day we pulled into Los Angeles, near Union Station, and beheld wide streets, low, flat buildings, and an expanse of blue sky such as I had never imagined could be seen on earth.

It was hot, and we were dazed, exhausted. But as I blinked around I became filled with a powerful feeling.

"Oh, Annie!" I hugged her to me. By the look on Annie's face, I knew she felt it, too.

I stretched out my arms, as if to draw in the very air. When we left New York it had been snowing; here it was warm, the air filled with the scents of warm earth and flowers.

The buildings were white. The streets were clean, without soot or smoke, without the hustle and the screech of traffic and the wailing of vendors and sirens—this was what Papa had wanted for us.

Along the streets grew palm trees of every variety, tall and thin, fat and round, some with fronds as wide as huge fans, others sleek and long. They swished in the breeze.

People here moved slower than in the East; the women's

clothes were brighter, the men opened their shirts at the throat and loosened their ties.

"It's so beautiful!" Annie exclaimed.

Mother, frowning, fussed about, gathering our luggage, and Father looked for a porter.

"Taxi!" Father called, motioning.

"We can't afford a taxi!" Mother snapped.

"Margo, for once let me manage!"

A taxi appeared; we squeezed in all our things, Annie and I sitting on Mother's and Father's laps.

Papa had sold our furniture in New York, and Mrs. Morgenstrom had lent him seventy dollars. The money was to last us until he found a job.

"Where to?" asked the driver.

"Hotel Rutledge," Papa replied.

"A hotel!" I exclaimed. We passed a beautiful hotel, with palm trees and vast lawns out front. I read the sign, THE AMBASSADOR. My heart raced.

The taxi sped past.

"Where's our hotel?" I asked. My voice shook.

"Stop worrying, Lisa," Mother scolded. "You don't need to know. The driver knows."

We pulled up in front of a brown building, miserably forlorn looking, the paint peeling, with a rusty balcony from which hung a battered sign: HOTEL RUTLEDGE.

Inside, a bald man stood behind a counter covered with red oilcloth, tacked down with brass studs. An odorous cigar hung wetly between his lips.

"We have two lovely rooms for you," the man said. "Bathroom down the hall. Hot plates in all the rooms— you can prepare food, but we don't allow any washing of dishes in the bathroom, do you understand?"

"But what about our things?" Mother asked, looking about.

"Things?" The man squinted at Papa.

"We have clothes, household things," Papa replied. "In boxes outside."

"Ha! This is a hotel, not a van-and-storage company."

Several sailors and young women came sauntering through the lobby, laughing. One of the girls tossed up her key, caught it again, and the sailor gave her a squeeze.

Mother reached into her purse for money. She looked ready to drop from fatigue. "Maybe you could bring our boxes in just for tonight," she said. "We'll be leaving in the morning."

The man took the dollar bills. Wordless, he went out to bring in our things.

"Who said we are leaving tomorrow?" Papa exclaimed, when the man was out of earshot. "We have reservations here for a week. We need time to find a place."

"We're leaving tomorrow," Mother said.

When she looked like that, even Papa didn't argue. "As you wish, Margo," he said with a formal nod. "We'll find another place tomorrow."

In the night we heard all sorts of noises. Down the hall a man and a woman were fighting. People laughed hysterically. Then they quieted down, and other noises followed. Groans and sighs, murmurings.

"What's that?" Annie whispered.

"I don't know," I said. I knew, though.

Later, there were mice scratching about in our room. Annie and I lay wide awake. "I have to go to the bathroom," she whispered. "But I'm afraid I'll step on a mouse."

"I thought you loved animals," I whispered.

"I do. That's why I don't want to step on it."

We laughed and laughed, holding our hands over our mouths so as not to awaken Ruth, who slept with us in the same double bed.

The next morning we were stiff and cramped, but we jumped out of bed, ready to go and begin exploring Los Angeles.

"They call it City of the Angels," Ruth told us, as we stood outside the dingy hotel waiting for our parents to take us away.

"It's because of the sky," Annie said. "Look at the clouds. They're all in puffy shapes. I never saw clouds like that in New York."

"A furnished apartment with a real kitchen," Mother was saying when she and Papa came out to join us.

"Very well," he said meekly.

"I don't mind following you all across the country, Arthur, leaving our friends, our jobs, taking the girls out of their schools, but when you take us to a hotel that is nothing but a . . ."

"Hush, Margo, the children . . ."

"I will find us a clean apartment on a residential street, where there are other families, decent people. . . ."

"All right, Margo. I understand. It wasn't the sort of place to bring . . ." Papa glanced at me. Our eyes met. His mouth twitched. He looked skyward, raised his brows, shrugged his shoulders.

I gave him a grin.

We found a furnished apartment that very day. It was called a "quadriplex," two apartments downstairs, two up. Our neighbors were quiet people, the landlord said. The lady upstairs seldom went out. The others worked. We saw nobody at all.

"What a genius your mother is, girls!" Papa exclaimed.

"Here less than twenty-four hours, and we already have a wonderful place to live. When she makes up her mind, she can do anything!"

Mother and Father stood in the middle of the living room, looking at each other, laughing.

"Forty-five dollars a month, Arthur," Mother said then, sobering. "That's a lot of money."

"Nothing is too good for my family," said Papa.

In the living room was a tiny fake fireplace with little gas jets in it. The other rooms had no heat. But then, it was always warm in California, wasn't it?

Everything sagged and creaked. The window screens were haphazardly patched. In the living room stood a sofa, one cushion ripped open, with yellowish stuffing pouring out. A small coffee table bore countless scars. But it was clean, and below the front windows, which were very near to the ground, grew hollyhocks and daisies. And outside, everywhere, there were trees.

The larger of the two bedrooms was for the three of us. It contained one double bed and two cots. We felt lucky; we'd use one of the cots for an extra couch.

The kitchen cupboards had glass doors, and there was a nook with built-in benches and a large wooden table. There was a little metal icebox with a wooden handle. Twice a week, the landlord said, the iceman came down the street in his truck, and we could buy a block of ice for a quarter, to keep our food fresh. Sink, counter, and stove were cracked from long use, but clean, and the kitchen had just been painted with a fresh coat of white. We could still smell the paint. It made up for the linoleum with its gouges and spots of rust. Off the kitchen was the narrow service porch, with its washtub, hot-water heater, and a few shelves.

The bathroom, to our dismay, was a wreck. Someone, in a fit of energy or destruction, had painted the sink a bright red. Green ferns alternated with gray stalks on the wallpaper.

Papa stared at the sink. His mouth twitched. "Better than a plain, white sink," he said. "The dirt won't show."

"We won't spend much time in the bathroom anyway," Mother said faintly.

"Maybe the landlord will buy us a new sink," I suggested.

"You're dreaming," said Ruth.

"We'll fix it up," Mother said.

Annie came running in, her eyes gleaming. "There's a garden outside. A real garden!"

We went out. Sure enough, some flowers grew in the small patch outside, bulky hydrangeas and daisies. A tree dominated the center of the grassy area, and a gracefully proportioned stone bench stood under the tree.

From the upstairs window I saw that a curtain had parted. A face at the window looked sternly down, an aged face, and gray.

From somewhere I heard a baby cry, just for an instant. Then it was silenced.

"Ruth, come and look at this!" Annie shouted. "It looks like a tiny dragon! Look! Look!"

Mother scolded, "No shouting here, girls! You must behave quietly. I don't want any trouble here." She looked about, as if we had offended someone.

"Mama, we just . . ." I began.

She cut me off. "I meant it, Lisa. No arguments!"

Ruth and I went to see the creature, which sat motionless on a rock. "It's a lizard," Ruth said. "He's watching us."

"So is someone else," I murmured, with a glance at the upstairs window. But the curtain was still. The figure had vanished.

We were quickly settled in school, and, oh, how we loved the warm days, the easy atmosphere. But Papa had trouble finding a job. He had wanted to work in a department store, selling coats. They said his English wasn't good enough. "Girls of fifteen and sixteen they hire!" he raged. "What do they know about coats and selling? I can sell a hundred times better, with my experience! What's to know for English?"

Mother had trouble, too. She signed up with an agency for work. They sent her out day after day to clean people's houses. Each day she came home weary, dispirited.

"Well, they kept me today, but they said they really want a Negro woman."

"Why do they want a Negro?"

"The lady said Negroes clean better."

"Are they crazy?" Papa ranted.

"Arthur, Arthur, please don't shout. I have another place tomorrow."

"I have a friend who is Negro," Annie said. "Her name is Janet. I love her."

"You love everybody," Ruth said crossly.

"We never knew any Negroes in Germany," Mother said.

"They're immigrants, too," said Ruth. "From Africa."

Papa laughed. "That was a long time ago."

"Annie," Mother said nervously, "I want you to stay home and play with your sisters."

We all knew Annie would do no such thing, but Mother had to say it.

For the next job Mama had to take three buses. She didn't get home until after seven and dropped into bed that night without even eating supper.

"Maybe I could get a job at a hospital," Mother said. "With babies."

As a young girl Mother had had training as a baby nurse; she had looked after little babies in a maternity ward before she was married. She had brought her certificate along, kept in a leather case.

The next day Mama did get a hospital job, but only for three days a week.

"Mama! You can be with the babies!" I cried, knowing how much she adored infants.

"No," she said. "They don't need anyone there. I'm hired—in the wards."

"What do you mean, Mother?" Ruth asked. "What must you do?"

"I'm a—a housekeeper," Mother said.

We asked no more questions. Three days' work a week meant that at least we could buy food.

Papa made the rounds. He went to the garment district. "Maybe later," people told him. "Now, we don't have any work. You have to get established first, meet people, have references."

So Papa went to work again as before, peddling neckties.

"It's fine," he exclaimed. "I get to meet people, important people in the garment industry. The buses are easy to catch, not like New York, with those terrible subways, and no snow under the feet. This is a piece of bread!"

"Cake," I said.

The grammar school was six blocks away. Ruth and I walked Annie to school in the morning, then caught the bus to the high school. After school Annie waited for us on the corner.

We'd been there just a few days when, as we headed home, we heard a commotion. Three high-school boys were walking behind us, hooting and howling.

"Ignore them," Ruth said in a low voice.

One boy bounded up, shouting, "Hey, you guys are German, aren't you?"

Ruth and I put Annie between us. We walked faster.

"I was talkin' to you!" the boy said, his tone insolent, threatening.

"Yeah," I replied loudly, swinging my arms. "We're German."

"I thought so," he said.

My heart was pounding with dread.

"*Heil Hitler!*" all three boys now shouted from behind us. They shouted, "*Zeig Heil! Zeig Heil!*" and laughed hysterically. They would never realize what anguish the name Hitler caused us. We hurried home.

Several days later, when Annie and I came home from the store, there on the stair stood an elderly woman, blinking down at us. She looked frail, and her hand gripped the railing, the purple veins standing out sharply.

"Good afternoon, girls," she said in a low voice that was deep and teacherly. "I am Miss McIvers. I live upstairs."

We introduced ourselves.

Miss McIvers looked at Annie for a long moment. Annie smiled up at the woman.

"Stay and talk with me a minute," the woman told Annie.

I excused myself and went to put our milk in the icebox.

A few minutes later, when I went out to look for Annie, she and the old woman were engrossed in conversation, something about the plants outside, the library several blocks away. ''You can take out six books at a time,'' Miss McIvers was telling Annie. ''I have a library card. You can get one, too.''

''But I don't have any money,'' Annie said.

''Oh, it's free. Absolutely free.''

''Free?'' Annie exclaimed. ''Lisa, it's free!''

''Maybe you will come up and read to me some time,'' Miss McIvers told Annie. ''You look like a smart little girl. I have known another little Jewish girl who used to live up the street. She was very smart, too.''

We watched the old woman make her slow progress up the stairs. It seemed an impossible journey.

Inside, Annie asked me, ''How does she know we're Jewish?''

''I don't know.''

''Do we look different?''

''I don't think so.''

''Act different?''

''Maybe. Or maybe the landlord told her.''

''How would he know?''

''Oh, Annie, stop asking questions. It is just one of those things we can't explain.''

Mother and Father talked about it that night.

''Maybe we should have moved to a Jewish neighborhood,'' Mother said.

''No. I don't want to live in a ghetto,'' Father said firmly. ''We have to learn to live with other Americans, all kinds. If people all stick together, only their own kind, they never grow.''

"We still have to grow, Arthur, at our age?"

They laughed. Then Papa said soberly, "I'm sorry the children have problems."

"Problems we have everyplace," said Mother. "Being alive is a problem."

"You are getting very wise, Margo."

"Life is teaching me, Arthur."

In my diary I wrote:

February 17, 1942. Papa told me about Fanny Brice, a Jewish girl who became very famous. We heard her on the radio. I saw a picture of her in a magazine, too, and she is so glamorous! If you're famous, people don't care what religion you are, or even what race. I wonder what Fanny Brice looked like when she was my age.

I am taking sewing again. I love my teacher, Mrs. Morgan. The sewing room is beautiful, with new machines. We are learning to make a peasant skirt. My teacher makes all her own clothes. That's what I want to do. She says you can have your own style, and that style is being different and not like everybody else. She says that's what makes people interesting. I wish I had a sewing machine at home.

Three big boys followed us home from school. I was scared. I didn't let them know it, though! Papa says some Jews live in a ghetto, all together, and they never have any trouble. I wouldn't want to live in a ghetto. If people never get to know each other, they are always enemies. The Werfels are Catholic, and without their help in Switzerland, I don't know what we'd have done. I even went to church with Erica once, and it was fine. If there is really only one God, what difference does it make how you pray to Him?

Maybe it would be better if there weren't any separate religions at all. If people were all the same, they couldn't hate each other, could they?

I'm going to make a little drawstring bag to go with my peasant skirt. I love things that match. Mrs. Morgan has the cutest outfit, a flowered skirt and a white blouse trimmed with the same flowered material. She has style.

Chapter 7

PAPA HAD PAID BACK Mrs. Morgenstrom, but then things got bad. Mother had to have a tooth filled. The stove needed repairs, and the landlord said Papa had to pay. Papa needed money to buy the ties that he peddled, and he needed shoes, for he walked a great deal and wore through the soles. "I can get a loan from the agency," he told us. "It's not charity. Just a loan."

Miss Shedley, the social worker from the agency, came to see us. She sat with her feet tight together, knees bared and toes rigid in beautiful high-heeled shoes. She wore a navy-blue suit with a large silver pin on the lapel, in the shape of leaves, and a white scarf around her neck. Miss Shedley had come to make a report about our needs.

"You understand," she said, "that these loans are interest-free, and are funded by several organizations. So we have to make certain that—uh—the need is real, and the money well spent."

"I understand," Mother said softly.

"How many times a week do you eat meat?" Miss Shedley asked.

"Two times." Mother replied. "Sometimes three. If there is a sale on hamburger, three times."

"Does Mr. Platt smoke?"

"Yes."

"That is a rather expensive habit," said Miss Shedley. She lit up a cigarette of her own, drawing on it like a movie actress. I rushed to get one of our glass-star ashtrays for her. She gave me a nod as she tapped her cigarette. I thought she was utterly fascinating—and horrible. In one way I longed to be like her, with long sleek legs, pretty shoes, and that fabulous silver pin. But she made me ashamed of my knees, of my stubby fingernails, and especially of my hair, which hung unevenly down, half-curling, half-straight.

"Well, I suppose one must have some vices," she added, laughing, stubbing out her cigarette.

"Papa rolls his own," I offered. "He has this little machine. Sometimes he lets me roll one for him." I had to be very careful not to spill out bits of tobacco.

"Well, isn't that nice," Miss Shedley said, giving me a stiff little smile.

Miss Shedley wrote something in her notebook. We three sat on straight chairs, watching her. Mother had said we must appear neatly dressed, combed, and quiet. Miss Shedley had been here for half an hour already; it seemed like an eternity. She had poked her nose into the kitchen, opening the icebox to study the food standing atop the block of ice. She had looked at the stove, then peered into our bathroom, saying "My, my" at the blood-red sink, then she swished through the bedrooms like an admiral making an inspection on shipboard.

Mother followed her, looking distressed, sighing a great deal, trying to smile.

"You have plenty of space," said the woman.

"Yes, yes. We are very satisfied," Mama said. She sighed.

"Have you found another job, Mrs. Platt? I understand" —she checked her notes—"that you work only three days a week."

"I am trying to get something else, too."

I felt sick. Miss Shedley was so cool, so pretty and unruffled, and Mama sat there in her housedress, her voice trembling.

"You have been trying, then? You have gone on interviews?" Miss Shedley's pencil was poised in the air.

"I went to a house yesterday," Mother said. "The lady wanted a nurse for her children. It is work I could do—I know everything about babies."

"Well?"

"She did not like it that I . . . my accent . . . she does not want a German woman. She thought, from the telephone, that I was Swedish. I took three buses. She offered me nothing. Not even a glass of water."

"Did she give you carfare home?" asked Miss Shedley.

"Yes."

"That is all they are required to do, Mrs. Platt."

Mother looked down at her hands. I felt a terrible, burning shame and anger. In Germany, Clara did all the cooking and washing, and Marie was hired to clean our house. Mama never had to do anything except look after us and help Papa entertain.

"Well, do you have other prospects, Mrs. Platt?" asked Miss Shedley.

Mother murmured to Ruth, "What means *prospects?*"

"Other opportunities," whispered Ruth, in German.

"Oh, yes," Mother said. She lifted her head, and now I saw a glint of pride in her eyes again. "I am going to see a lady tomorrow. She lives in Carthay Circle. A very nice house, I think. A nice neighborhood. She wants someone to clean her house two days a week."

"Well, that's fine," said Miss Shedley. "Do your daughters work?"

"No. They go to school."

Miss Shedley pursed her lips. "I mean weekends. After school. We don't want to foster dependence, Mrs. Platt. People have to help themselves."

My face burned.

"How was your last report card, Ruth?" Miss Shedley asked.

"In New York I got all As," Ruth replied. "Here . . . the gym teacher said I will fail if I don't get some tennis shoes. We have to have tennis shoes for gym."

Miss Shedley drew herself up, her chest high. "Well, you should go to work if you need tennis shoes. You are immigrants, after all. You cannot expect other people to give you everything."

"I'm sorry," Ruth murmured. "I did not mean . . ."

"Agency loans are not for shoes. Not for frills. Only for rent and food."

She rose. Several papers fell down around her. Annie, staring, had to be poked by Mother and told, "Go pick them up!"

"You're a good little girl," said Miss Shedley.

When she had gone, Mother laid her head back against the sofa. The small room was hot and stuffy. We sat there, the four of us, motionless and silent.

After a moment I ran into the kitchen for a white towel. I wound the towel around my neck as I rushed to Mama's closet and got into her high-heeled shoes and old blue jacket. Back in the living room, I paused to make my steps precise, my bearing stern.

"Mrs. Platt," I said, in imitation of Miss Shedley, my tone slightly nasal and high-pitched, "you know we have no money for shoes here! Don't you know in America people only go barefoot? And—what is that? Are you wearing a brassiere? My, my, you should know the agency's money is not for such trivialities, not at all."

"Mama's brassiere is not trivial," Ruth cried, shrieking with laughter, and Mama, too, was holding her sides.

"Ah, Lisa, you are a comic." Mother sighed. "What a terrible woman! Well, we are rid of her. Let's celebrate."

"Celebrate?" we cried. "How?"

"For dinner, chocolate soup," said Mother, going to the kitchen to get out the pots.

Chocolate soup was absolutely delicious, and a meal in itself. Mother used to make it for us in Germany, with tiny macaroons on top. It was hot and creamy and chocolatey.

"Where can we get macaroons?" I wondered.

"We'll make them—somehow," Mother said.

I don't know how she did it. The taste was in our mouths all night, warm and delicious. Even Papa loved it, though he was usually a meat-and-potatoes man.

"What are we celebrating with chocolate soup?" he asked. "Did I forget a birthday?"

We all laughed, and I got into my costume again and

played Miss Shedley, the Social Worker, and reveled in the laughter I raised.

Mama got the job at Carthay Circle. I'd ridden past there on the bus. The houses were large, some with fountains out front, and some even had swimming pools.

At home, we surrounded Mama, plied her with questions. "Is the house beautiful? Is the lady nice? What is her name? Are there any children?"

"It is Mrs. Grant," Mother said. Mother brushed back her hair with her hands. She had worn the same housedress to her job that she always wore at home, and the same old shoes, run down at the heels.

"Tell us about the house!" we cried.

"It's a house," Mother said shortly, "with a roof, beds, and a toilet, just like ours."

"Are there children?" Annie wanted to know.

"Two. A girl your age, eight, and another one, a little older than Lisa."

"Are they nice?" Annie asked.

"Annie, go set the table and stop asking so many questions," Mother snapped. She turned to me. "Did you go to the grocery store like I told you?"

"Yes, I did. I brought back change."

"Good. And did you go to the school to get our sugar ration books, like I told you?"

"Yes! I always do what you tell me," I exclaimed.

"Don't be so fresh!" Mother snapped. "You think that because we are in America, I am going to let you behave like an American child, without any manners, talking back. . . ."

"Who is talking back?" Papa strode into the house. "Did you get the job?"

"Yes, I got the job."

"Wonderful! Did they give you lunch there?"

"Yes, a chicken-salad sandwich and some leftover mousse."

"My God! Chicken salad! Fancy, shmancy."

Still, Mother seemed upset. We couldn't figure out why she was so cross. After all, she had a fine job in a beautiful home, and had to take only two buses to get there. And she made five dollars a day. She showed me the money after the dishes were done.

I said, "My teacher wants us to buy savings stamps. To help the war effort. When you fill the book, you get a war bond worth twenty-five dollars."

"Lisa, every day you come home with something different," Mother said, "and it always costs money."

"You always want to know what is happening at school," I grumbled. I felt cheated. Unappreciated.

"If things are so bad," Ruth offered, "I'll quit school and get a job."

"Don't you dare ever let me hear you say that again!" Mother snapped.

Papa called, "Margo, come hear the news!"

"Margo, come here! Go there! What's the matter with all of you?" Mother cried, tossing down the dish towel. But we all went into the living room, for the radio drew us like a magnet every night, with news of the war.

The news always left us feeling shaken. Every night, talk of battles in the Pacific—we were losing the war over there. Next, the Japanese might cross the ocean, invade Hawaii, then California.

In Europe, our men were dying, too. We at home were asked to increase our efforts, to save gasoline and tires, to give up vacations, to honor the rationing system and not hoard food. Every day the requests increased; every night the news was still bad.

When it was over Annie said, "My new friend, Setsu, is going to help me plant a garden."

Setsu's family lived next door in a wood-frame house with a wide porch out front.

"Where will you get the seeds?" Mother asked. She seemed to brace herself against more talk of money.

"Setsu is giving me the seeds. They have extra. They have a big garden with all kinds of vegetables."

"I suppose that would be a good thing," Mother said, though somewhat dubiously.

"They call them 'victory gardens,' " Ruth said.

"Yes," Papa nodded. "If people plant their own vegetables, the farm produce can be sent to the troops overseas. I see."

"I'm going to plant beans and peas and tomatoes and squash."

"Quatsch?" Mother asked, laughing. It was the German word for "nonsense."

"Squash. It's very American," Annie replied. "You eat it with brown sugar. Setsu's mother gave me some to try."

Mother whirled around, alarmed. "What? You are eating at other people's houses?"

"They are our neighbors," Annie said. "I've been playing with her every day. And we can walk to school together. Ruth and Lisa won't have to take me anymore."

"A whole group of kids Annie's age walk together," I told Mother.

Mother stood back, shaking her head.

"Margo, I'm sure everything is fine," Papa said.

"Setsu is in my class, too," Annie said excitedly. "She is so sweet, and they have a little baby. . . ."

"Setsu? I never heard such a name," Mama exclaimed. "Who are these people? Why didn't you ask me?"

"You were not home!" Annie cried. "What's wrong with having a friend? She's Japanese. Her name means . . ."

"Japanese?" Mama looked from me to Ruth. "Did you know our neighbors are Japanese?"

I shrugged. "So what?"

"I—I don't know. I have never lived with Japanese people. And they eat squash? I thought—I thought Japanese people only eat rice and fish. What is their religion, Annie?"

"I don't know," Annie said miserably. "What's wrong? Can't I have friends? Why are you so . . . ?"

"Quiet!" Mother snapped. "I will find out about these people. You will not decide where you go, what you eat, who you play with, do you understand? I am not so American yet as to let my children run wild and do whatever they please."

We went to our bedroom. When Mother came in to kiss us good-night, she was still cross. "This place is a pigpen!" she said.

"We'll clean it tomorrow, Mama," Ruth said hastily, putting away a few things.

"And another thing," Mother said. "Every night before you go to bed, I want you girls to wash your own underthings. In the summer you will hang them out on the line to dry. If it is raining, you will hang them on the service porch."

"Why do we have to do it every night?" Ruth asked.

"Because I never, never want you to expect anyone

else to do this for you. Some things are personal and private. You will do it, all of you, even Annie, starting tonight. And one thing more. I never want to hear you calling grown-ups by their first name.''

''We never do!'' Ruth exclaimed. ''Why are you so mad?''

''Don't answer me back, either, young lady!''

''Yes, Mama,'' we said.

In the bathroom Annie stood at the sink, scrubbing her panties. I did mine in the tub.

''Setsu is the prettiest girl I ever saw,'' Annie said. ''And they have the sweetest little baby boy, and a gray cat that never even goes outside. Why's Mama being so mean?''

''She hates her job,'' I said.

That night I wrote in my diary:

March 1, 1942. Sometimes Mama is so prejudiced, it makes me furious! I have seen Setsu's brothers at school. They nod and say hello, because we are neighbors. They are quiet and very polite.

I feel sorry for Mama, though. I hate to think of her cleaning other people's dirt, even toilets. Tonight I told Mother I'd get a job after school, but she wants me to stay home and take care of Annie. Then she said I'm spoiled because I'm always wanting things. I was only trying to help her, but she wouldn't listen. I feel like I'm always mad at Mother, and then I feel bad, because she works so hard. Her hair is turning gray. I think she should dye it. I told her so, and she got mad again.

Oh! I met the sweetest, cutest girl in my sewing class. Her name is Sheila Kestner. She has very black, curly hair, and she wears beautiful clothes. They live on Swath-more Drive. Sheila thinks I'm smart and clever. She laughs at my jokes and impersonations. We're going to take the bus tomorrow after school and go to Hollywood to look at the shops. I told Sheila how much I want to dance and to take lessons. She said there are lots of dance studios in Hollywood. Sheila said I can sleep over at her house some time. I can't wait!

Chapter 8

MARCH 2, 1942. Sheila and I went to Hollywood. It was so wonderful! We looked in the shop windows at all the beautiful clothes. We stood outside the Grauman's Chinese Theater, where movie stars go for opening nights. I told Sheila I long to dance in the movies, like Ginger Rogers, and Sheila listened. She didn't think it was a silly idea. Sheila wants to be a teacher. Ruth got a job tutoring some high school seniors in German. She makes seventy-five cents an hour!

Sheila and I went to two dance studios. At one they wouldn't even talk to us. At the other, lessons cost five dollars an hour, and you have to audition. I felt so stupid and awkward there. A group of girls came out, all in their leotards, laughing together. They were wearing toe shoes, and they looked so wonderful. Even if I could take lessons, I'd have to have shoes and a costume and everything, and I hate to ask Mother and Father for money. I wish they'd *let me work! Maybe after I turn fifteen. My birthday's only a month away!*

Later that week, when Mother came home and said, "I have a surprise for you, Lisa," I thought she had a present for me. In Germany, Mother always used to go shopping weeks ahead of time for our birthday gifts. She could never wait to give them to us.

Ruth and I went into the living room, where a large cardboard box stood. "What is it?" Ruth asked.

"Clothes," said Mother. "They were Andrea's, Mrs. Grant's daughter. They said we could have them."

Tears of disappointment stung my eyes. Looking down at the box, I concealed them. As we went through the clothes, I poured gratitude and enthusiasm into my voice, feeling virtuous and kind.

The clothes really were nice. Ruth and I went through them in disbelief. Sweaters, skirts, blouses, all perfectly good, no holes or stains. One sweater was blue with little alpine flowers knitted in, and silver buttons. There were a couple of dresses, various knee socks, some matching, some not, and of all things, a pair of tennis shoes. The right shoe had a hole on top, where the big toe went. The laces were frayed and knotted together. Ruth put the shoes on, squeezing in just a little, and she smiled widely.

"I'll bet you a dollar," she said smugly, "that now I'll get all A's on my report card."

We divided up the clothes. I washed mine carefully with Lux flakes and laid them on a towel in the shade to dry. They smelled good and fresh; now I could imagine that the things were new. I could not understand how Andrea

Grant could possibly part with such beautiful things—unless she had grown out of them. Yes, I told myself, she must have grown a great deal, and now they no longer fit. Lucky me!

I wore the sweater with the little alpine flowers and silver buttons to school the following week. I felt so pretty setting out that day! All during classes, it seemed that people smiled at me; clothes make a difference, I thought happily, vowing that someday I'd have a closet bursting with beautiful things.

At lunchtime, I hurried through the halls to meet Sheila; after lunch we had sewing. I planned to ask the teacher about making a skirt to go with the sweater, something in light blue. Sheila and I loved talking about clothes.

I hurried through the crowded halls, when suddenly I felt a weight on my shoulder. I turned. There was a girl I'd never seen before, blond and pink cheeked, wearing a beautiful red cashmere sweater and matching plaid skirt.

"You must be Lisa Platt!" she shouted.

"Yes—I . . ."

"Your mother's our maid," she said, still louder. "Margo. I recognized you because you're wearing my sweater!"

"Hey, that's her sweater!" shouted a couple of boys, laughing. "Take it off! Take it off!"

And they started to sing a popular ditty:

"Take it off, take it off,
Cried the boys in the rear—
Take it off, take it off,
That was all you could hear . . ."

Andrea's face seemed to dissolve before my eyes.

Suddenly she screamed out, "Hey, Brenda! Wait up!" and disappeared into the crowd.

I ran to the girls' lavatory, where I felt my stomach heaving, and the sour taste rising into my mouth.

I leaned over the sink, washed my face with cold water again and again, but I could not stop the anger, the shame.

I came into class late. Sheila whispered to me, "Where were you, Lisa? What happened? I thought we were eating together."

I shook my head, unable to speak, ashamed to tell her what had happened. After class, when she asked me again, I kept my eyes down as I lied, "I was in the nurse's office, Sheila. I was sick."

Mother didn't get home until late that afternoon. I had started supper, a meat loaf, which I hated, because it stuck to my fingers.

"What a day," she said, first thing. "Mrs. Grant had me do all the ironing. She kept me nearly two hours extra. Because she gave me those clothes, I guess. Lisa, did you make the beds?"

"Yes, I made the beds."

"And did you take Annie to the library like I told you?"

"Yes! I always do everything! Why didn't you tell me that Andrea Grant goes to my school?"

"I didn't think about it. Why? Do you know her?"

"Oh, yes," I cried angrily. "I sure know her now. Do you know what happened? I was never so humiliated in my life."

I told it in every detail. Mother sat down on the bench in the nook, staring at me. Her face looked very pale; even her eyes seemed washed out, red rimmed.

"I'm sorry," she whispered at last. "I'm sorry you were embarrassed."

"You should have told me. I wouldn't have worn that sweater. She sounded like I'd stolen it! She was blaming me for having it! I was so embarrassed, I thought I'd die. Do you know what it's like to have somebody come up to you, pointing, yelling out that you're wearing their clothes? I felt like a thief. I felt . . ."

"There is nothing I can do about it now, Lisa."

Papa worked late that night. Our lights were already out when he came into the bedroom and touched my shoulder. "Lisa!" he whispered. "Are you awake?"

"Yes."

"Come into the living room," he said. "I want to talk to you."

I slipped out of the double bed and followed him into the living room.

"Your mother told me what happened at school today," he said, "about the clothes."

"Oh, yes, Papa," I exclaimed. "I was so humiliated! It was so awful, Papa, you can't imagine. Mama should have told me she goes to my school! I shouldn't have been put in such a position," I cried, warming up to my complaints.

"You think it is your mama's fault?" Papa leaned forward, rolled himself a cigarette, lit it. He drew deeply, fanning away the smoke as he said, with narrowed eyes, "You know, Lisa, nobody can humiliate you. You can only do that to yourself. I saw those clothes your mother got for you. I know she had to carry that whole box of clothes home on the bus. From the bus stop she had to walk four blocks with it to this house. She did it gladly.

For you and Ruth. And this is how you repay her? I'm ashamed of you. I want you to apologize now to your mother.''

"I won't!'' I cried, remembering that scene with Andrea.

My father had never struck me before. But I felt his hand hard against the side of my face, only once, and I saw a look on his face that I would never forget.

The next day, when I looked in my closet, the sweater with the little flowers, and the skirt and the other things were gone.

I got up the nerve, at last, to ask Mother about it.

"Your father has packed those things away,'' Mother said. "He will give them to you in due time. When you have earned them back, he said.''

As the days went on, I said nothing to Papa about the clothes. I was too ashamed. Then one day I found some of the garments on my bed with a note: "For helping Annie with her homework . . .'' and the next day some more, "For washing all my socks . . .''

Of course, I wore the clothes to school. I never talked to Andrea Grant again, and she seemed not to know that I existed. Nor did Mother ever bring home anything else from that house.

Through Sheila Kestner I met Louise and Janine, and soon the four of us were hanging around together.

My friends were exciting and so very American, at least Sheila and Louise were. Janine came from England. We all adored her accent. She'd been sent here by some agency after her parents were killed in one of the bombing raids over London. Janine had been away at school in the country, so she was saved. You'd think Janine would be miserable and gloomy, but she wasn't. She lived with her grandparents.

Janine told me about Miss Klausenstock's ballet class.

"A ballet class? Here at school?" I was amazed, excited.

"It's a gym elective," Sheila explained. "But old K. is so mean nobody wants to take the class."

"I do!" I exclaimed.

"You won't when you see her," said Sheila grimly. "She's awful. A real dictator. German, you know. Oh— sorry. I didn't mean . . ."

"I'm not insulted," I said, smiling. "I don't consider myself German—at least not like the Germans still over there."

Janine said, "I started her class, and I quit."

"She's that mean?" I asked.

"Well, I just couldn't keep up," Janine said, pushing back her long blond hair. "I'm not a very good dancer. But you—you look as though you'd be wonderful. Have you danced before?"

"For five years in Germany," I said with some pride.

"Oh, then you'd make the class for sure," Janine said. "You have to try out."

"How do I see this dictator?" I asked.

"She has an office in the gym," my friends told me. "She hates Jews. The Jewish kids call her 'the Nazi.' "

That day at noon I made my way to the gym. I found the teacher in a cluttered little office, nothing more than a cubicle carved out of the hallway. I could see the dark brown roots of her poorly bleached blond hair as she bent over her desk.

I stood there, getting up my courage to tap at the glass, when she looked up suddenly and barked out, "Well? For heaven's sake, don't just stand there, can't you talk?"

"I—yes. I wanted to ask you . . . my name is Lisa Platt," I said, beginning again.

She gave me a sarcastic grin. "Oh, you wanted to ask me that your name is Lisa Platt? Oh, very interesting. What is the matter with you?"

"I'm a dancer," I whispered.

"What?"

"A dancer!"

"What do you want?" she shouted.

"I want to join your dancing class," I said loudly, my heart jumping in my chest.

She stared at me for a long moment. "Where have you danced before?"

I swallowed, hard. "I studied with Madame Lotte Zimmerman in Berlin," I said.

The word *Berlin* brought a flicker to her eyes, but no expression to her face. "How long?"

"Five years."

"When did you stop?"

"I—I haven't danced ballet in over three years."

"And you call yourself a dancer?" she cried.

I shook my head. "I need to practice."

"Most certainly," she snapped. "You may practice in the gym early mornings and after school. After a few weeks, *if* you think you can still dance," she said pointedly, "I will audition you for the class."

I nodded, my chest feeling tight, my throat constricted.

"Don't wag your head at me like a goat!" she barked. "What do you say?"

"Thank you, Madame Klausenstock," I said, for I knew very well that all dance teachers like to be called "Madame."

I turned.

"Did I dismiss you?" she called.

I faced her once again, eyes straight ahead, my face burning with hatred, resentment, need. I needed to dance!

"Don't think for one moment," she said, "that you will get any special favors from me just because you are German. You may go."

I felt so strange all that day, elated and devastated at the same time. I told Ruth about it that evening.

"All the kids say she's a Nazi," I fumed. "What's she doing here in America? Why do they let her teach?"

"You shouldn't believe everything you hear," Ruth said.

"She yelled at me, just because I wanted to dance."

"You shouldn't be so prejudiced," Ruth said.

"I'm not prejudiced!" I shouted.

"Shut up, you guys!" Annie called from the floor on her side of the bed. "I'm doing my math."

All night I slept a troubled sleep, turning, fighting, dreaming. I woke up very early, found Papa in the kitchen drinking coffee all alone.

"Good morning!" he exclaimed, speaking softly. "Have a roll. Coffee?"

I smiled. "I don't drink coffee, Papa."

"I was just thinking what a wonderful morning it is," he said. "Do you hear the birds? Nature . . ." He sighed. "Nature is a wonderful thing. How the birds exist, how every creature knows . . ." He broke out of his reverie. "It reminds me of my youth," he said. "We lived in a little village, you know, and the neighbors kept chickens."

"Do you miss Germany, Papa?" I asked.

He paused, then shook his head. "No. This is my country. I hate them too much to miss anything." He sipped the last of his coffee. "I have to go."

"So early?"

"Can't be too early," he said with a smile. He picked
up his large case of neckties, bending under its weight.
And I thought, if Papa could get out so early, so could I.

I got to the school just as the janitor was opening the
gate, and in the gym I practiced at the bar for a whole
hour.

Afterward I felt the pinch in my waist, the pulling in
my calves. I remembered the age-old dancers' admonition:
If you fail to practice for one day, you'll know the difference.
If you fail to practice two days in a row, the audience
will know the difference.

From that day on I went to the gym first thing every
morning, working out my own routine. First, the bar exer-
cises. I could see myself in the mirror, and I commanded
myself, as Madame Zimmerman used to instruct us: *Relax.
Smile. Bend. Stretch. Easy, farther, bend, stretch.*

My legs were limbering; now arms had to follow, hands
positioned and graceful, while face remained calm, and I
remembered to breathe. Breathe! *Down, two, three, four,
stretch, stretch hold. Over, two, three, four . . .* In my
mind I heard my beloved teacher's voice, counting out
the movements, always light, friendly, but firm. "Now
step away from the bar!"

Three steps. I imagined music, three-quarter time. *Point
front, point side, point back, second position, again. Again.
Hands relaxed, arms up, head high, chin up, buttocks tight!
Now again, watch your hands, two, three, together, eyes
up, sweep that toe, point, point . . .*

On and on I practiced, feeling the warmth in my body
and music in my mind.

I never saw Madame K., as I now called her to myself
and with the other girls, but one morning, when I was
trying some turns, I slipped and fell flat on the floor.

That afternoon, when I was coming out of the gym after a later practice session, the teacher was there in the doorway, tapping her cane on the floor. Coldly she said, "There's a box of resin over there in the hall. You should know enough to look for it!"

Before I could say anything she had disappeared. I hated her! But I loved to dance more.

Mornings in the gym became the high point of my day. I began to try my old routines again, felt myself flying, leaping, whirling, loving life.

"Lisa, you've got color in your cheeks again!" Papa said happily at suppertime.

"She is dancing," Mother told him, smiling.

Dancing not only gave me joy, it brought back a part of my life that I had shut away. How I had loved lessons with Madame Zimmerman! She not only taught us the dance, she talked to us about life. "The dance is not isolated from life, my children. To dance is to live! And when you are dancing, use your entire body, your entire spirit, not the feet, the hands, the head, the arms, like separate parts cut off from each other—no! Every movement and every thought must be part of the dance. Think of your technique constantly, constantly, when you are eating, playing, working, sleeping. But then, my children, when you are really dancing—then, think only of the dance."

Now, after so many years away from my teacher, I finally began to understand her.

Chapter 9

I WAS STARTLED ONE DAY, returning from school late, to see Mother and Annie outside on that bit of sidewalk exactly between our quadriplex and the house next door, where Setsu lived. They were talking together, the two women and two girls. The late-afternoon sun through the maple trees overhead sent flecks of light down upon the little group. They looked to me like figures in a painting.

As I came closer I saw Setsu's mother, her sleek black hair gleaming in the sun, wearing a blue embroidered smock over gray trousers. Her movements were delicate, her features serene. Beside her my mother gestured, moved, bobbed her head as she talked. Setsu and Annie stood close together, smiling. At one point their hands touched. I did not want to interrupt, for they were talking so earnestly, and then I saw the little carriage with the baby in it, and as I approached I heard my mother saying, "I was a baby nurse in Europe. I love babies. What a sweet little one!"

"Would you like to hold him?" asked Setsu's mother.

"Ah, you don't want to wake him if he is sleeping!" my mother objected, though even from this distance I heard the longing in her voice.

"Baby likes to be held," said Setsu's mother, and I heard Setsu give a little giggle. It was then that Annie touched Setsu's hand.

The mother bent down, gently took the baby with his blanket from the carriage, and put him into Mother's arms.

Something in my mother changed completely in that moment, the way I suppose I changed when I was truly dancing. Mother's head bent down to the child, her arms clasped it to her breast, and her entire body curved in an arc that was pure grace and protection and love. She stood thus, slightly swaying, rocking, moving in that unconscious way that trees move in the wind.

"Ah, what a sweet one, so soft, so beautiful. A big boy for his age! Is he eating solid food?"

"Milk," said the mother, smiling broadly. "He eat also from little jars," she said proudly. "Spinach. Carrots. Sometimes I make myself, from garden."

"Oh, what a beautiful, healthy child. And Setsu, too, is a beautiful little girl."

Setsu, in immaculate pink cotton, beamed.

"Your Annie," countered the Japanese mother, "good girl, so nice, always polite manners in our house. We glad she be in our house with Setsu."

"It is good the girls are friends," Mother said. She gazed down at the baby again. I saw her profile, gentle now, all struggle gone. Slowly she gave the little baby back to his mother.

"We happy to see you," said Setsu's mother.

"Likewise," said my mother. It was a new term for her; she said it with confidence.

That night I awakened to the sound of sirens.

My heart pounded as I lay in bed for those terrible moments, waiting for bombs to drop from the sky.

Ruth was sitting up in her bed across the room. A tiny flashlight beam pierced the blackness in our room; she had been reading under the covers. Papa had long since taped our windows with butcher paper. Not a single ray of light must be allowed to escape, perhaps to guide enemy bombers to a target.

I sat up, stunned, waiting. The sound of airplanes rumbled overhead. Beside me, Annie slept soundly. I watched her waken, stiffen, her eyes on the ceiling while she waited, as I did, for the whistling sound that a bomb makes when it falls, the inevitable explosion, then fire. We had seen this many times in the newsreels and movies. The seconds lengthened. I expected to die.

"Ruth!" I called.

She leaped out of her bed, came into mine. We lay very close together. I marveled at her toughness. "I'm scared!" I whispered.

"It's all right. Probably just a drill."

"What if it isn't?"

Ruth and I had been down to the beach when we first arrived in Los Angeles. It had seemed like a marvel to see the dark-blue waves pitching high over the sand, and we had stood gazing out to the horizon, trying to imagine the lands that touched the opposite shore. Japan, that small place on the map, curled like a caterpiller, Japan touched the Pacific Ocean, too, and could launch submarines and planes and fighting men. Ruth and I had been to the beach again two weeks ago; the shores were fortified with rolls of barbed wire, and sentries patrolled with guard dogs. Children no longer played in the surf; the beach looked like a wasteland.

"Arthur, don't leave us!" Mother's voice was high-pitched, anxious.

"I must," Papa said firmly. I heard his footsteps. He came to our door, fully dressed and wearing his Air Raid Warden cap and badge.

Papa stood at the door like a soldier ready to leave for duty. With his German accent, he sounded like a parody of Hitler and all the evil ones; how could they have made *him* air-raid warden for our block? It seemed ludicrous.

"Put out that light!" Papa shouted now to Ruth. Ruth instantly obeyed.

We heard the front door slam, while still the sirens rang out, and then we heard trucks begin to roll along the street, and we imagined soldiers moving into battle position. We lived only twenty miles from the Pacific Ocean. If Japanese submarines landed there, we would be invaded, maybe imprisoned or killed.

Suddenly I felt Ruth's arm around me. I felt her warmth.

"I'm scared," I whispered again.

"Everybody is," she whispered back. "What you have to do is pretend you're not."

I felt a surge of love for my sister. Just yesterday she'd wanted to borrow my blue sweater; I'd said no. Now I told her, "You can wear any of my clothes that you want to, Ruth."

"Thanks," she said. "But what about tomorrow? When you're not scared?" I could tell she was angry, for she trembled slightly.

"What's wrong? Are you still mad at me about yester-day?"

"No. I just wish," she said in a low voice, "he wouldn't go out there like that. People laugh at him. He gets every-thing all mixed up. He acts like—I don't know. I just get so embarrassed."

"About Papa?"

"About Papa!" she mimicked in a sugary voice.

Mother came in, carrying a candle, which she shielded with her hand. Her hair was down.

"Ah, girls. At least the four of us will wait together," she said. But there was harshness in her voice.

Annie began to sing one of the many war songs we learned at school:

"From the halls of Montezuma
To the shores of Tripoli
We will fight our country's battles
On the land and on the sea. . . ."

Annie expected us to join in, as everyone did at school during an air-raid drill. But Mother, Ruth, and I just sat there on the bed in the dim light of the candle, and then I felt Mother gesturing beside me.

"How can he rush out and leave us like that?" Mother said angrily. "Men! They think war is a game. Oh, they claim to want peace, but as soon as they hear the sirens and the horns, off they go. They are all alike. He runs out with his cap and his badge, all excited, leaving us here alone. What if there really is an attack? The men go off to their games. It is the women who are left alone to repair the damage."

I had never heard Mother talk against my father before. Her vehemence stunned me. Combining with Ruth's anger, it made me feel that somehow I'd lost everything, all the love and closeness of before. Emergencies ought to bring people together, I thought, my own resentment rising. I imagined Setsu's family sitting together. Annie had told me that their plan, for air raids, was to gather together underneath their great, heavy dining-room table.

"What do they do under the table?" I had asked Annie.

"They sing songs. About the Yanks and the Seabees."

I gave Annie a nudge and launched into the Marine Corps hymn. She immediately joined me; I harmonized. Ruth started to sing, too, and I could see, as our voices blended, that Mother was watching us in the flickering candlelight, her features composed again.

At length we heard the "all clear" signal, a long, single tone. Mother boiled water for Postum. Coffee was hard to get, so we drank a substitute.

"There's a rubber drive at school," Annie reminded us.

"I already gave our rubber mat," Mother said. "Maybe we have something else. I'll look."

Mother gathered up the cups, put them into the sink. "I went down to the Red Cross yesterday," she said. "I heard at the hospital that they need volunteers to help with blood donations."

"When would you have time?" I asked. "You already work at two jobs."

"One night a week, I have time," she said. "I told them I have a daughter," she added. "They want young girls to help serve coffee and doughnuts to the servicemen. Also, sometimes they want a pretty girl to talk to, while they give blood. It helps them forget about the needle.''

In that instant I pictured it all, me wearing a white smock and a little cap, being kind and helpful and so very pretty as I gave refreshments to servicemen who were far from home. . . .

''If you have the time, Ruth,'' Mother continued, ''I want you to go with me every Tuesday night.''

I took a deep breath. ''What about me?''

''You're too young, Lisa,'' Mother said firmly. ''Anyway, I need you to stay home and take care of Annie, in case Papa is working late.''

Tears sprang to my eyes. I tried to bite back the harsh words, but I couldn't. ''Why do you always choose Ruth?'' I cried. ''Why am I always the one who has to stay home with Annie? Why can't I ever do anything that's fun?''

''Fun!'' Mother cried. ''What's fun got to do with it? We all have to help the war effort in any way we can, and for you to take care of Annie while we do war work is just as important as what Ruth and I will do. . . .''

Ruth gave me a lofty look that said, ''So there!''

''How can you say that?'' I sputtered. ''Just a few minutes ago you said that war is just a game for men, and now you take Ruth to work at the Red Cross, while I . . .''

''Lisa!'' My mother stood before me, furious. ''That's enough! I never said the war isn't *important*. We have to do everything we can to win, don't you understand that? We have to defeat those monsters. Have you any idea what the world would be like if they win? Slaves, that's what we'd be! Except that we—you and I and all the other Jews— we would be dead. They are rounding them up, packing them into cattle cars, gassing them, burning the bodies in ovens. . . .''

"Ovens?" Annie gasped. I saw two red splotches on her cheeks, as if she'd been slapped.

Mother sat down. "It's the truth. I can't shield you from it. I won't! You have to understand."

We got ready for bed again. Of course, we couldn't sleep. Annie kept turning, tossing, sighing.

At last I got up and put on the small light. "What's wrong?"

"Nothing," she said, toneless.

Ruth was under the sheet, reading by flashlight. She had learned to tune us out.

"I got some new nail polish," I told Annie. "Pearl pink."

"That's nice."

"Tomorrow I'll let you use some. We'll do your toenails."

"We don't have anybody here, you know," she said morosely.

"What are you talking about?"

"My friends. Setsu and Janet, they all have families. Aunts. Uncles and cousins. They all get together. They have grandparents, too. They all have dinner together and they talk and they sing and play games."

"We did that, too," I said softly, "in Germany."

"I never did."

"Yes, you did. You were too young to remember."

"Then it's just as if I never did," she insisted.

"That's true," I agreed. "But you heard Mother," I added. "We all have to help the war effort. You have to help, too."

"How?"

"By not complaining about not having a big family,

and by being good, collecting things—you know. I'm sorry
for what I said about not wanting to stay with you. I like
staying with you.''

"I know. I am good," she said. "And I'm getting tough.
People think Jews are weaklings. I'll show them!''

"Tough?''

"Yes. I'm the fastest runner in third grade.''

"Congratulations," I said. "How'd you accomplish
that?''

"Mostly practice. Setsu and I run away from the Mexi-
cans.''

"They chase you home from school?''

"Not always," Annie said. "About once a week. They
call Setsu a dirty Jap.''

"And you?''

"Oh, I don't listen. They jump up and down and yell,
'Sheeny, sheeny, killed my Lord.' They're so stupid. I
never killed anybody!''

"So you guys run?''

"We run faster than any of them!'' Annie said, grinning.
Soberly she added, "I wish the Jews in Germany would
run. Why didn't they all just leave like we did? Why didn't
they run away?''

"I don't know.''

Ruth put out her flashlight. We all lay quietly for a
while. I heard Annie's breathing, and Ruth's.

"I'm giving my kickball for the rubber drive," Annie
said. "Setsu is giving up her rubber doll and they're even
bringing in the baby's bath toys.''

"I'll take my curlers," I said.

"I'll give my girdle," Ruth said from her bed in the
dark.

"What?" I giggled explosively. "I didn't know you had a girdle!"

"Mother gave me one," Ruth said. "Actually, it feels awful. It's like iron bars around your middle."

"I'll take it to school for the war effort," Annie said, stifling a laugh.

We heard Papa come in. "All clear!" he announced.

"Shh, Arthur! The girls are trying to sleep."

We heard them talking. "They spotted some more enemy U-boats off the coast . . . oil on the beaches . . ."

"They could land here . . . be in the city in no time. . . . They caught one of them with a whole case of color flares and signal rockets. It would be easy for a spy to signal the Japanese from our beaches. . . ."

"Good-night, Ruth," I said.

"Good-night, Lisa," she replied.

"Good-night," said Annie.

It was the last night we three ever slept in the same room together.

Chapter 10

Nọт ᴌᴏɴɢ ᴀꜰᴛᴇʀᴡᴀʀᴅ, Papa brought home a sewing machine.

"Lisa!" he called that afternoon. "Lisa! Come here at once."

I rushed out from the bathroom, where I'd been washing my hair, trying to bleach it with lemon juice. I was still dripping when I saw Papa directing two Mexican men, who grunted as they labored over the weight of a huge factory sewing machine, complete with built-in worktable and a black iron treadle.

"Where put?" one of the men muttered.

"In her room," Papa said, pointing.

I ran ahead, stood in the bedroom, dumbfounded.

"Push the beds together," Papa directed. "Move the bureau. Take that chair out, you don't need it. Ah, that's fine, fine. Put it down."

There stood the machine, an ugly monstrosity, and there

stood Papa, his arms outstretched, beaming. "I got it for a wonderful price," he said. "Mr. Kline was going to junk it."

"But, Papa," I murmured, "our machines at school are small, they are entirely different. I don't know whether I can sew on such a large machine."

"Tut, tut," said Papa. "You're an intelligent girl. I know you can learn to use this machine. I heard you telling your new friend that you want to make your own clothes. Now you can."

"I guess I could try," I said.

"You have to buy material," Papa said. "Maybe I can get it for you wholesale." He seemed to be waiting for something.

"Thank you, thank you, Papa!" I exclaimed, and ran to give him a kiss.

He patted my back. "Where is Annie?"

"Probably at Setsu's."

Thoughtfully, he nodded. "They are our neighbors. I don't even know what the man does."

"Everyone is always busy here," I said. In Germany Mother and Papa used to go out often, meeting friends in the cafés. On Sunday mornings we sometimes met other families in the park.

"They don't bother anybody," Papa said thoughtfully. "I wish . . ." But he turned away again. "I have to go back to work," he said. "I only came to bring you the machine."

When Ruth came home from school and saw the sewing machine in our room, she let out a shriek.

"Impossible!" she cried. "There's hardly space to walk! How can I work in here? That thing is a dust catcher.

It'll always be in the way. It probably makes a terrible
racket, and when Annie comes in here with Setsu, jabber-
ing . . .''

I had an idea. "Suppose we have Annie sleep on the
service porch?''

Ruth's face lit up. "You mean . . . would she?''

"We could put her bed in there. Make it cozy. Give
her the throw rug.''

"And a little table, this chair . . .''

"We'll arrange all her toys,'' I said. "She won't mind.''

"She'll probably love the privacy. I mean, you and I
stay up much later. She can never get to sleep.''

"When we listen to the radio, she won't be yelling,'' I
added.

"And I can bring my friends in and have some privacy,''
Ruth said. "Let's do it now. It'll be all done when she
comes home. She'll see how nice it is.''

"What about the window?'' The window was barred,
ugly.

"Well, when you learn to sew on that machine, you
can make her some pretty curtains. I'll help you pay for
the material.''

Suddenly I was doubtful. "Maybe we should make
the curtains first, then tell Annie, show her how nice it
is.''

"No,'' Ruth said firmly. "I want to do it now, while I
have time. I've got a school project . . .''

"All right.'' Still I hesitated. "We should ask Mother.''

"Mother's at work. She won't care. We're not doing
anything wrong.''

"All right.''

We hurried to move in the furniture. Then we spread
out Annie's dolls and stuffed animals up on the windowsill,

the bed, and atop the wooden board that covered the deep gray-metal washtub.

"The washtub in her bedroom doesn't look so good," I murmured, surveying our handiwork.

"We'll put a cloth over it," Ruth said. "It will be okay."

"She won't like the water heater and the pipes."

"She won't even notice."

"All right."

I sat down at my new machine. It had its own little light. Papa had also left me a little pile of scraps. I took a scrap, just for practice. "Zipppp!" The machine raced as I lightly pumped the treadle; I could sew an entire seam in less than a minute, once I learned control over this monster.

I made a potholder with crisscross stitching, practicing my skill with the new machine, ripping, repairing, concentrating.

I did not hear Annie come in. I heard only her gasp.

Out in the hall Ruth told her, "We've fixed it all up for you, honey. It's so cute! Look, we've put your toys out, and your dolls on the bed. . . ."

Annie said nothing. I saw her face at the door, though, her eyes upon me as she watched me sitting there, sewing. "You moved me out of the room," she said. "*Both* of you."

The look on her face left me speechless. I had always been Annie's friend, her protector. If Ruth didn't have time for her or got cross with her, there was always me. Annie counted on me.

"Annie," I began, "I didn't mean to make you feel . . ."

But she had vanished into the service porch, closing the door behind her.

That night Mother and Father went directly to their English class. Ruth and I fixed a supper of peanut-butter-and-jelly sandwiches. Annie took her sandwich into the yard. She sat on the stone bench, eating and reading. Later Setsu came out, and the two of them went to Setsu's yard to play.

By the time Mother and Papa came home, we were all in bed. I was reading a novel, *How Green Was My Valley,* which Ruth had gotten from the book club. The book club was Ruth's only real extravagance. It was a rare occasion that Ruth let me read one of her books before she was finished. I thought how well we were getting along together.

Mother came into the room and looked around at the machine, at me. She said, "Do you know what you two have done to Annie?"

I shook my head, yawning, appearing unconcerned, while in reality I felt a twisting pain in my stomach.

"She didn't care," Ruth said.

"The room was too crowded," I added.

"You didn't even ask her," Mother said.

"So what? She's always in the way," Ruth said. "She's so messy. And she brings in her friends. . . ."

Mother stood there looking at us, her expression grave. "You girls have to learn to get along," she said. Her gaze rested on me. "Maybe Annie will forget this," she said, "but you never will."

Later I got up, went to the service porch, knocked on the door.

No answer.

A night-light shone under the door. I realized that in her entire life Annie had never slept alone before. Inside me, the twisting felt like a worm in my gut. "Annie!" I whispered. "Can I come in?"

I opened the door. She lay there bunched up on her side. She would not turn over.

"All right, then," I muttered. "Good-night."

Ruth and I went to Sears and bought some material. I did make curtains for Annie. But Mother was right. The guilt stayed with me. Annie didn't come into our bedroom at all. A coldness seemed to have washed over her, a layer of solemnity.

And then came the terrible blow.

It was early on a Sunday. Annie came running into the house, screaming. "They're leaving! Everything's packed. All the furniture is gone! Setsu didn't even talk to me. She didn't even say good-bye. She left in the truck with her uncle. They're all being sent away someplace to the desert—why? Why?"

"Heaven help us!" Mother stood up, hands raised. "That poor woman and the baby—oh, what a terrible thing, to be chased out of your own home!"

"Where are they going? Why so suddenly?" I asked, perplexed.

"The Japanese are being sent away," Mother said. She did not look at any of us.

"They could be spies," Ruth said.

"Setsu's not a spy!" Annie screamed.

Papa, halfway through shaving, came out at the commotion. "What's going on?"

Annie sat in the kitchen nook, sobbing. "They've taken Setsu away. Just because she's Japanese. It isn't fair!"

"Annie, Annie." Papa sat down beside her, put his arm around her. "Poor Setsu, it's too bad she had to go, but her family . . ."

"Where are they going? They didn't want to leave their house! Setsu's mother was crying."

"They'll be sent to . . . to camps," Papa said. "So they can all be together. Until the war is over."

"You knew this!" Annie cried, accusing. "Why didn't you tell me? Why didn't you do something?"

"Child, what can I do? Be reasonable. It's up to the government. The president. Annie, this is wartime. People have to make sacrifices. We have to be careful. We don't know which Japanese are loyal and which are spies. So all of them have to leave the coast—do you understand? If even a few of them were spies, they could destroy this country. Don't you see?"

"No! No! I want Setsu back! She's my friend."

"When this war is over," Mother said, "then . . ."

"The rotten war will never be over!" Annie shrieked. "It's horrible. It makes people mean and bad. I hate it! I hate everything."

"You don't hate your papa, do you?" Father crooned.

Annie looked at him, glaring. She did not reply. I knew she was thinking of the sewing machine Papa had brought, what it had done to her life, and now this.

"She'll get over it," Papa said later, when Annie was outside in the garden again, sitting alone on the stone bench.

"No, she won't," I said.

I went outside, stood on the sidewalk. Next door the large wooden house stood empty. I could see it by the windows; windows have a way of looking sad when a house is alone. Neighbors stood around in small clumps, shifting their weight the way grown-ups do when they are embarrassed, when they know they have to say something.

"I say good riddance," one woman flung out. Her hair was done up in curlers; her face shone with cream or sweat.

"If they hadn't of left," said another, "Bruce was gonna rout them out anyhow. We don't want Japs in this neighborhood."

Apart from the women, the men talked together while they smoked their cigarettes. Every time one made a statement, the others rumbled and nodded and shifted their feet. Sometimes they laughed. Mostly they frowned, and they flipped their cigarette butts out into the street.

". . . don't believe everything you hear, it's all propaganda," one of them said.

"They say that with Mussolini in power, at least the trains run on time!"

Laughter, like an invisible net, bound them together.

"It's the Jews themselves invented those stories," said another, "all about concentration camps and those ghastly murders. Nobody would do things like that."

"A Nazi is still a human being," said another.

"Listen, if you ask me, it's all a pack of lies, to get sympathy. The Jews just want to come in here and take over, like they always do."

I went around to the backyard. There was Annie, squatting over her victory garden.

"How's it doing?" I asked. I knelt down beside her.

"The beans are the best," she said soberly, touching several little green leaves with the tip of her finger. "Those ferny things are carrots. Corn over there. Squash."

"That's really beautiful," I said.

"I wish I had more space. I'd plant everything—tomatoes, potatoes, everything. I wish I had a farm. I wish we could move away to a farm, far away, maybe to Australia."

"Maybe Setsu will come back," I said.

"It wasn't fair," she said.

That same week Papa came home and said he had finally met a man who was willing to go into business with him. "His money," Papa declared proudly, "my brains."

"His money, you mean, and your sweat," Mother said grimly.

"It's the same thing."

"What will you do, Arthur?"

"Make ladies' coats and suits. Eventually, fur-trimmed things, like I made in Germany."

"Would women wear fur in this climate?"

"Women who can afford fur will wear it anyplace," Papa replied with a smile. "But that comes later. First, I'll make some samples, show them around. I'll take orders, and Mr. Miles will give me the money to have the coats made up."

"Why does this Mr. Miles want to give you money, Arthur?"

"He likes me," said Papa, hands outstretched. "Besides, we'll share the profit. We met at the delicatessen. I showed him your photographs. We talked. I showed him my designs, some sketches on the tablecloth . . ."

"The tablecloth! Oh, Arthur."

Papa was always drawing on tablecloths, napkins, even the wall.

A week or so later Papa came home with a large garment bag over his shoulder. Inside were two coats, one beige and one red—samples.

Ruth and Mother tried them on to show us how beautiful they were, and Papa stroked the cloth, straightened the lapels, shook his head in admiration over his own handiwork.

"One hundred percent wool," he said proudly. "I'll

sell it for eighteen ninety-five. Look at those gorgeous buttons! Expensive buttons, and they'll never fall off, never.''

"Are we going to be rich, Papa?" Annie asked.

Papa pursed his lips, lit a cigarette. "Rich? No, Annie. We have debts to pay back first. It takes a long, long time to get rich. It takes a long time just to catch up, to make a decent living.''

When Papa said we would soon move out of the neighborhood, none of us was sorry. Papa was looking for a house to rent, one with a separate garage where he could work. In the new house we would have a telephone, too!

Prosperity was just around the corner, Papa said.

My birthday was on April 11. In my diary I wrote:

Annie gave me a beautiful blue fountain pen for my birthday. She has been saving her allowance for ages, I guess. She gets only ten cents a week. Mother was right; I feel so awful every time I think of what we did to her. I have looked through my diary, and how much I have written about the war. Mother says, if we children can't even get along, how can nations? It's true. I guess even if people were all the same nationality and the same religion, they'd still find things to fight about. Because the truth is, everybody is selfish. Like me. I usually feel good on my birthday. Today I feel rotten.

Mother gave me five dollars for my birthday, and a lovely little purse she bought for herself and never used. Ruth gave me a cloth-covered diary. This one is nearly full.

A terrible family moved in next door. They are so loud! They keep a junked-up old car out on the front lawn. Mother says they are Polish. She says the Polish are low-class. I don't know what to believe anymore. I feel like crying, but I won't, because they say that if you cry on your birthday you'll cry every day of the entire next year.

I hope we can move soon.

Chapter 11

GOOD NEWS seemed to come all together. At the beginning of May, Sheila had a slumber party. Janine, Louise, and I were invited. I'd never had more fun in my life. We laughed half the night. I did movie star impersonations; they loved it!

The very next day, before school, just as I got started practicing at the bar, there stood Madame K. "You may join my advanced ballet class," she said. "I have been watching you. You are, at least, faithful."

"Thank you, thank you, Madame!" I breathed.

"Do not think," she continued sternly, "that you will be in the front row. I have some very talented dancers in that class. You will have to work hard to keep up with them."

"Yes, Madame," I said demurely, my voice soft, while inside I was bursting with excitement. Advanced class! All day the joy of it sang through me. And when I told

them at home, everybody beamed and clapped. Then Papa
told us his surprise.

"I have found a house for us. It is in a nice neighborhood.
Closer to your school, Lisa and Ruth. And it has a separate
garage."

"Will we buy a car?" Ruth asked eagerly.

"No. I will use the garage for a workshop. The coats
will be sewn at the factory, but I'll do some finishing in
the garage, and I'll pack the coats into boxes and make
out my bills there."

"Tell us about the house!" we begged. "Is it pretty?
Is there a yard?"

"Wait and see," Papa said, smiling mysteriously.

The following Sunday, a rattletrap old truck waited on
the curb while two men loaded our household goods. The
biggest thing was my sewing machine. Mother fussed about,
sweeping out the kitchen, cleaning the icebox, locking windows.

"Annie!" Mother called again and again. No answer.

"She must be up there with Miss McIvers," Mother
said, exasperated. "Lisa, go and get her. Go on! The truck
is nearly ready to leave."

Reluctantly I went up the stairs. I had never been in
that apartment, nor had I ever seen anyone go up there,
except for the milk deliveryman and Annie. I shuddered
as I knocked at the door, bracing myself against the musty,
rotten smell I was certain I'd encounter.

I knocked again, louder. No answer.

Then I heard the sudden, rich tone of music. Beautiful
music.

I knocked very hard.

Annie came to the door, looking startled and flushed,
as if she'd just been awakened from a dream.

"Who is it, Annie?" called Miss McIvers.

"It's my sister."

"Tell her to come in then, and for goodness sake, close that door!"

I walked as softly as a mouse across the carpeted floor, toward the large overstuffed chair where Miss McIvers sat, her knees covered with an afghan. Phonograph music filled the room, the beautiful voices of a woman and a man singing a love duet. I stood, transfixed, imagining the two of them in the moonlight, standing on a balcony overlooking the sea, falling in love.

A delicate fragrance hung in the air, eucalyptus leaves and lavender, I think. The carpet was beige, the furniture pale rose.

When the song was over, we three remained silent. The room was shadowed, soft.

"Annie, we have to go now," I said. My voice sounded husky.

"Take the record, Annie," said Miss McIvers. "Take it with you. As a keepsake."

"Really?" Annie gasped. She took the record, put it into its sleeve, then carried it close against her chest.

"You've been a good girl, Annie," said the old woman. "And a good reader. Go to my purse now and take your ten cents."

Annie went to the table, opened the bulging black-leather bag, took out a dime.

"Thank you, Miss McIvers," she said. She drew close to the old woman, touched her hand. "Good-bye, Miss McIvers." Formally she added, "It was nice meeting you."

"Don't you worry!" Miss McIvers said, with sudden energy. "We will surely meet again."

"I know," said Annie.

Outside, the sunlight blinded me for a few moments as we walked down the stairs.

"What did she mean, you'll meet again?" I asked Annie.

"Oh, Miss McIvers believes that time is on a continuum."

"What?"

"She believes that time is relative, that events happen not in a straight line but . . . it's hard to explain. It's sort of like everything comes around, nothing in the world is ever lost. Like souls. She's very interested in reincarnation, and in Albert Einstein."

"She talked to you about things like that?"

"Oh, we talked about lots of things," Annie said lightly, skipping down the stairs.

Mother stood at the curb, gesturing. "Arthur! Where in heaven's name is that man?"

Annie grabbed my arm. "Come with me."

"Where?"

"To the backyard."

We went out to look at the plants that grew there in the sparse soil. "I just wanted to remember it in my mind," Annie said. "My very first garden ever in the world. I told Miss McIvers she can have it."

I glanced up, thought I saw a hand at the upstairs window, and felt a small sense of loss.

"Wasn't that record beautiful?" Annie asked. "And wasn't it nice of Miss McIvers to give it to me?"

"Yes. But we don't have a phonograph."

"Oh, someday we'll get one. Then I'll hear this record every day."

"What's it called?"

"*The Student Prince*. That song we heard is so beautiful.

It's called 'Golden Days.' " She started to sing: " 'Golden days, in the sunshine of our happy youth . . .' "

"That's nice," I said.

"Lisa," Annie asked earnestly, "do you think these are our golden days? Are we in the sunshine of our happy youth?"

I laughed, but only for a moment. Then I pondered. I thought of all our problems, Papa working day and night, Mother seldom home and always tired, and never enough money.

"We might not be in our golden days yet, Annie," I said. "But maybe these are our silver days."

"Silver days," Annie mused. "Yes. I like that."

The driver was gunning the truck's motor now. Mother had disappeared, probably looking for Father, scolding. Ruth waited on the curb, twirling her hair through her fingers while she read a book and snapped chewing gum in her teeth.

"Where'd you get the gum?" Annie cried. "I haven't seen any gum for a year!"

Wordless, Ruth reached into her pocket, gave Annie a piece. "Hush," she said. "I'm reading."

Annie broke the piece in half to share with me. Gum was rare, a part of the war effort; we didn't know how. If any of us got a piece of gum, we saved it in a wrapper overnight or stuck it on a bedpost or the bureau to be chewed again.

Mother and Papa came out. "Why did you have to get into the bathtub just when the moving truck arrived?" Mother scolded.

"I like to begin life in a new place all nice and clean," Papa replied. He smiled at us all around. "Don't be angry,

Margo. Come, let's go. What are we waiting for? Don't you know we pay this fellow by the hour?''

We three sat in the back of the truck with the boxes and bundles. We drove for fifteen or twenty minutes, stopping at last in front of a house with a wide porch, bounded by lavender lantana bushes in full bloom.

It was a house, a real house separate from all others, nothing attached, nothing to mar its privacy.

Ruth got out, gasped. "Look at the porch! We can put a hammock out there.''

"Look at the flowers," Annie squealed. "Look at the palm tree! We own a tree! We have a tree. Is it ours? Did we buy it?''

"No," Papa said. "We are renting. Sixty-five dollars a month.''

It seemed like a huge sum. We were impressed.

"Wait until you see the backyard," Mother said happily. "It's the best part of the house.''

We ran into the backyard, saw the huge olive tree, the lawn with space to run and play, the garage at the end of the driveway, softened by thick stalks of calla lilies and geraniums.

We ran back out to the front, up the porch, nearly tripping over the man who carried our things inside, then through the house with its living room, dining room, nice big kitchen, and two bedrooms.

"It's a palace!" Annie exclaimed, arms outstretched.

"Where do we sleep?" Ruth asked.

"Look," Mother said. She led us to a room just behind the parlor, a room full of sunshine. "This used to be a sun porch, but now it's a bedroom. I thought Ruth might like to have this room to herself." She turned to me. "Since she is the oldest.''

Annie stood looking at me. Her face was solemn.

"We can share a room," I said. "We'll be roommates."

Annie said, "Are you going to paste up pictures of movie stars all over the walls?"

"Sure!"

"Oh, Lord," Annie groaned. "And I guess you'll have that sewing machine in there, too?"

"You guessed right."

"Well, I guess I can stand it," Annie said.

"What about beds?" Ruth asked. She stood facing Papa, her hands on her hips. "Have you forgotten to get beds for us?"

"No, young lady," Papa said, imitating her stance, her voice. "I have not forgotten anything. At three o'clock the truck is coming with our new furniture. Beds and tables and chairs and everything you will need. The things are not exactly brand-new, but . . ."—he gestured with his arms—"very nice. Much better than orange crates."

Papa started work each day before any of us was even awake. Often I'd go out to the garage after school and watch him work. The garage was crammed with cartons of buttons, bits of woolen cloth called "swatches," papers and pencils, fashion books, telephone books, labels, shipping boxes, hangers, and coats.

Coats hung in the front closet off the living room. More coats hung on a rack that Papa moved from one room to another, and finally out to the garage.

He called us together one day in the living room.

"Sit down, everyone," he said. Papa's face was solemn, but I could see the twinkle in his eyes, and his movements were pure joy and pride. "I have something to show you."

"What is it, Arthur?" Mother objected. "I have to fix dinner."

"Sit, sit. Don't be always in a hurry. Take it easy." Papa was picking up slang in the factory. "Everything will be hunky-dory."

He reached into the front closet, brought out a coat, bright red with a collar of lustrous black fur.

He held up the coat, turned it from front to back, spread it over his knee, stroked the long fur with the back of his hands, blew on it to separate the hairs, then brushed it down again, so we could all see how the fur glistened. He opened the coat to display the rich red lining, the beautiful, even hem, then showed us the stitching on the pockets.

"What do you think?"

"Gorgeous," I breathed.

"You are a genius, Arthur," Mother said.

"Can I have one?" Ruth asked.

"Look at the design!" Papa said gleefully. "Look at that workmanship! It is all hand-finished, not a thread extra, and buttons in tight, they will never fall off. Never. What do you think costs such a coat? What?"

"A hundred dollars!" Annie shouted.

"Sixty-five," I offered.

"Forty-nine ninety-five," Papa declared. "Including the fur. Nobody in the whole country can make a coat so good for this price. Nobody. Only Arthur Platt. Look. I have my own label."

He had saved this for last. Onto the sleeve was sewn a satin label that read, ARTHUR PLATT—100% WOOL—MADE IN THE USA.

Now, I thought, aching with pride, we had really, really arrived.

"You love it?" Papa asked.

We all nodded, and in unison said, "We love it."

"Now comes the sixty-four dollar question," Papa said. "Who wants to go into business with me? Who wants to work with me? Be a real partner?"

"What do you mean, Arthur?" Mother frowned. "What do you want us to do?"

"Nothing too hard. It is child's play." He pointed to Annie. "A nine-year-old child can do it."

"I can even thread my own needles," Annie said.

"Ha. See? I want you all to learn to sew linings into the collars. You can sew labels onto sleeves. And when that is done, we go over every inch of the coat to clean it up, cut off extra threads, make it perfect."

"I'll do it," I said, nodding. "I've been getting good at sewing."

"This is very careful work," Papa said.

"I'll be very careful."

"I can do it, too," Annie said.

For a moment Papa looked doubtful. "Yes—maybe you can. You are smart enough. . . ."

"But little fingers . . ." Mother began.

"We'll let her try," Papa said. "And everybody gets paid the same. Fifty cents per collar. Ten cents per label. Fifteen cents cleaning up the coat. Okay?"

"Okay," we all said.

"Not me," Ruth said. "You know I can't sew."

"Won't you even try?" Papa exclaimed.

"No, she can't, Arthur!" Mother said angrily. "Everyone isn't alike. She doesn't have to sew. Ruth is—fine without sewing. She helps me at the Red Cross, she makes bandages and wraps packages and talks to the blood donors. . . ."

"I'm sorry!" Papa said, hands raised as if to ward off an attack.

Ruth said, "I have something to tell all of you, too."

"What?" Papa regarded Ruth with interest.

"When I graduate next June," she said, "I am planning to go to City College. Don't worry," she added quickly. "I'll get a job and pay for my tuition."

"College?" Papa exclaimed. He pondered, shook his head, then slapped his thigh. "College!" he cried, exalting. "My God. Imagine it, my daughter a college student, maybe a graduate . . . you want to study to be a doctor?"

"Papa, you never listen!" Ruth complained.

"What? What am I doing wrong? I will help you become a doctor. . . ."

"I don't want to be a doctor, Papa. I want to be a nurse. I've wanted it all my life."

Papa shook his head at Mother. "All her life she has wanted this? Why didn't anybody tell me?"

"She's telling you now, Arthur."

Suddenly I felt cheated. She hadn't told me, either.

Papa went to Ruth. Solemnly he kissed her forehead. "Be a nurse, my child," he said. "It's a good thing, taking care of sick people. Yes. A fine thing."

I looked at Ruth, so grown-up, taller than I, self-assured. No wonder all the boys thought she was terrific. She had goals.

That night I asked Papa for a piece of satin lining.

"What do you want with this?" he asked.

"I want to make a dance skirt. I only need a yard and a half."

"What color?"

"Blue would be nice."

"How about red? I have a remnant."

"Great!" I exclaimed.

"It costs one dollar," he said.

"Are you kidding, Papa? You are going to sell me this? You won't give it to me?"

"Sew two collars, you earn a dollar," he said.

"All right."

"I'll give you credit," he said grandly, cutting off the material, rolling it up for me, a real professional. "You can have a couple of weeks to pay me. Okeydoke?"

"Okeydoke," I said.

Chapter 12

THAT FALL Mother and Father joined a club. The members were all Jewish immigrants from Germany. It wasn't anything fancy, with dues or a building, just a group of German Jews who hired a hall once a month for a get-together. I realized, after Mother and Father came home from one or two of these gatherings, how they must have missed having friends who spoke their language and had the same memories. Days afterward, I'd hear Mama humming some old German tune. "Ah, the old songs are the best," she'd murmur happily.

One Sunday Will Alexander came into our lives. He was the son of another club member. When the doorbell rang, Mother called for Ruth to answer it. "I'm expecting something from the club," she said.

"Tell Lisa to go," came Ruth's voice from the bathroom, where she was applying leg makeup, a substitute for nylons, which were impossible to get.

I went to the door. A boy stood there, a young man, really, about Ruth's age, with dark hair, wonderful dark, snapping eyes, and the nicest smile in the world.

"Hello," he said, smiling. "I'm Will Alexander. My parents asked me to deliver this."

He held out the envelope. I took it and stood there, unable to think.

"I just came to bring this," he repeated. "It's a club list." He looked embarrassed. "I was in the neighborhood anyway."

Then, suddenly it dawned on me why he had really come. His next question confirmed it. "Are you Ruth?" he asked.

"No, I'm Lisa, her sister."

"Oh!" He seemed relieved, glancing around.

Mother appeared just behind me at the door. "Will! It's nice of you to bring us this. Won't you come in?" Mother gave me a slight nudge. "Move, Lisa!"

Stupidly, I was blocking the door.

"Sit down, Will. How are your parents?"

"Fine, fine, Mrs. Platt, thank you."

I thought, if he'd had a cap in his hands, he'd be twirling it around.

"I would like you to meet my other daughter, too," Mother said.

Will smiled expectantly.

"How about some iced tea, Will?"

"That would be nice, Mrs. Platt."

"Excuse me," Mother said. She was breathing heavily.

Ruth came in, looking beautiful as always. Her legs looked tan and sleek with the makeup. Her dark hair was perfect, softly curled around her face, and she had used *my* lipstick. I had always wanted to look like Ruth; I realized this now so suddenly that I felt an ache in my stomach.

Instantly Will rose to his feet. His color changed. So did his voice. "Hello! You must be Ruth. . . ."

Miserably I mumbled some excuse and went out into the kitchen.

"You can take the tea to him," Mother told me. "Isn't he a nice boy?"

"I wouldn't know," I said crossly. "How can I tell just by looking?" But I felt struck with a dull ache, a sick feeling.

I went in with the tea and set it down. Will was talking animatedly about his car. ". . . a real beaut! She goes sixty-five miles an hour, but of course I can't take her that fast, and now with gasoline rationing . . . Want to go for a ride, Ruth? I'll take you to Griffith Park."

"I guess so," Ruth said, standing up.

"Here's your tea, Will," I said, handing him the glass.

He took a sip, smiled at me. "Thanks, Lisa."

Ruth stood at the door. "Well, do you want to go, then?" she said.

"Sure!" Will set down the glass and rushed to open the door for Ruth. "Bye!" he called hurriedly, and then I heard the car door slam, the engine start, and they were gone. I decided to go over to Janine's, hoping she was home.

The streets were quiet, for it was Sunday, and most people who were going someplace for amusement had already left. I thought of Ruth at the park. With Will. What must it be like to be with him alone?

When I got to Janine's, I knocked softly at the door. Her grandparents didn't like noise. They were nice people,

but as they often told us girls, "We don't know about
young folks; our own children grew up and left us ages
ago."

Janine came to the door, laughing when she saw me,
saying in her gentle but very English way, "I'm overjoyed
to see you, Lisa! I was so bored, really, and I longed to
talk to someone—that is, not just anyone, you understand—
come in! I'll fix us a cola. I've got a couple of new movie
magazines—want to look at them together? Come on, then,
oh, this is fun."

I greeted her grandparents, who were reading the paper
in the parlor. Janine and I went to her room. It was a
beautiful room, with everything matching, and several cut-
glass perfume bottles on the bureau, a mirror, a carved
coatrack on the wall, an extra chair with pretty cushions—
luxuries, all.

I felt a pang of envy, then remembered about her parents
and realized I was glad to be me.

We sat down on her hooked rug. The wood floor glistened.
On Janine's desk was a vase with two roses in it.

"I love your room," I breathed.

"I got a new perfume. Want to try it? It's called Tabu.
Very sexy." Janine laughed, dabbed some perfume behind
my ears, while I admired the bottle and the scent.

"I just saw the cutest boy ever," I said.

"Oh? Walking over?"

"He's with my sister. Took her to Griffith Park."

"Uh-oh," said Janine. She always understood. "So,
what are you going to do? Just be miserable? Or will you
fight for him! Yeah, that's the ticket, put up a fight. What's
he like, Lisa?"

"Darling. Dark hair, dark eyes, taller than me—about

five-eight or -nine, I'd guess. He wore gray pants and a pale-yellow shirt, open at the throat, no tie—he had loafers on, gray socks, argyles. I wonder who made him the argyles?''

Janine laughed. "You certainly are observant. Anything else?''

"I think he was wearing one of those ID bracelets. You know, with his name on it.''

"How long did you say you were with him?''

"About three and a half minutes, I'd say," I replied, grinning. "He really came to see Ruth. That thing about the club was just an excuse. You know how the folks are, always trying to arrange things for Ruth. You'd think she was twenty-five and needing to get married.''

"How old is this Prince Charming?''

"I'd guess eighteen. He's gorgeous. He has a car. He talked about it. . . . Ruth was hardly listening.''

"So, that's the ticket," Janine said, clapping her hands gleefully. "You learn about that car. Be enthusiastic. Listen, I read an article all about how to get a man. You must show him you're interested in the things that please him, be a good listener, not a talker. . . .''

"But I'm not interested in cars," I objected.

"But you must pretend to be.''

"That's not sincere!''

"Whoever said you had to be sincere, silly! You just get him interested. Get him looking at you. Then, when he really looks into your eyes, sees your smile, why, he just goes and falls for you, that's all. He moves closer. He reaches out. He touches your arm. Pulls you to him. His face is very near yours. . . .''

We both burst out laughing.

"Let's do you!" Janine exclaimed.

"Okay!"

She rushed into the bathroom, came back with a box of cosmetics, eye creams, rouge, lipstick, dark pencils, pancake makeup, and face powder.

We spent the next hour making each other up, laughing uproariously, until Janine's grandma came by, peeked in, and threw up her hands, calling, "Good gracious, what next?" when she saw our richly decorated faces.

"Doesn't your grandma mind you wearing makeup?"

"Poof, she doesn't care. Why should she? Long as I'm a good girl."

"Are you?" I teased. Janine was almost sixteen, and she seemed experienced.

"Yes," she said seriously. "Tell you what. Only been kissed once, that's me. One time, by a guy that worked at a pub down the street from our flat in London. Oh, he was grand, though. Of course, I pushed him away. I was only fourteen. I still think of it. I do. You ever been kissed like that, Lisa? I mean, like making you feel silly and shivery all over?"

"No," I said. "Never like that." I sighed. "Truth is," I said, "I've never been kissed at all."

"Ah. Well, we have to change that," she said. "Wouldn't it be grand if this handsome bloke, this Will, were the first?"

"Yes."

"When might you see him again?"

"I don't know—if he comes to see Ruth. Wait—there's going to be a club party later this year, Mother said. We'll all go. Mother said there's even going to be a talent contest. She said I ought to enter it."

"Well, if you entered the contest," Janine exclaimed, "he'd have to notice you then, wouldn't he? And if you won the prize . . ."

"The prize is three whole dollars," I said.

"Fabulous! Three dollars and a man all at the same time!"

I laughed. "Oh, Janine, you're the limit." Instantly I reconsidered. "I can't do it."

"Why not? Scared?"

"I'm not scared to dance! I'm making a dance skirt, but I'll need a top and tights and new shoes."

Then suddenly, something was settled in my mind. On the way over I had passed a bakery with a sign out front.

"I'm going to get a job, Janine," I said firmly.

She looked at me, wide-eyed. "Really? Why, that's swell. Really keen," she said, and I wondered whether she really meant it or just felt sorry for me.

That Monday afternoon I went down to the bakery where I'd seen the sign, HELP WANTED.

"Do you still need someone to help?" I said timidly.

The baker looked up, grumpy, nodding. "You want a job? Aren't you a little young?"

"I'm fifteen. I could work on Saturdays," I said.

He thought this over. "Saturdays? You an early riser?"

"Yes. I always get up by six A.M.," I said stoutly, though that was a gross untruth; what I always did was lie in bed until at least nine o'clock, listening to "Let's Pretend" with Annie. It was her favorite radio program.

"Well, I could sure use somebody to open up early, get out the goods on Saturdays. You willing to be here at six?"

"What do you pay?" I boldly asked.

"I can start you at thirty-five cents an hour. And on

Saturdays there's bound to be some leftovers. Doughnuts. Can't keep those over to Monday, they get stale.''

"Jelly doughnuts?" I asked, my mouth watering.

He grinned. ''You got it!''

He explained the job to me. I was to come in early and wipe out the cases, clean the glass counters, put out the rolls and cookies and cakes for display. After that, I'd help the bakers wash the pans until the store opened at eight-thirty, at which time I would wait on customers alone until the owner and his wife arrived at ten. I'd go home at three or four, depending on the number of customers.

I swiftly calculated what a fortune I'd make. Over three dollars every week!

When I left, he gave me a sack of jelly doughnuts. ''To seal our bargain,'' he said.

I rushed home. Mother was still at work, but Papa was in the garage talking on the telephone. I waited until he was finished, then offered him a jelly doughnut and told him about my job. He looked at me intently. ''You want to work on Saturdays? Isn't it enough that you are sewing collars for me?''

"I can sew on Sundays and a little in the evenings," I said. ''Please let me take the job, Papa. I need the experience. I'm old enough now.''

He ate the doughnut in three bites, licked his fingers, then lit a cigarette. ''Your mother wants you to have time to study. And still to play. I remember when I was young. I had very little time to play at all. Very little.''

"I don't need to play, Papa! Anyhow, working at the bakery will be fun. I get to put out the cakes and sell things and make change.''

"Fun?" He smiled. "At first it is fun, I suppose," he said thoughtfully. ''Well, you should have a chance to do what you want. To learn something. Whatever you learn, it comes in handy later.'' He put out his cigarette. ''You're a good girl, Lisa. I'll talk to your mother.''

Somehow it was settled, and that night when I went to tell Mother good-night she kissed me tenderly and said, ''I'm proud of you, my Lischen,'' using her old pet name for me. ''Just don't think that making money is the only important thing in life.''

I suppose we had all thought that once Papa got into the coat business and we got jobs, everything would be easy. We still had to watch every penny. It seemed as if I never had the right clothes, or enough of them. The girls at school wore matching sweaters and skirts, fuzzy-topped socks and new-looking saddle oxfords. One girl in my social studies class had fourteen cashmere sweaters; I counted them.

I remembered with a pang how Mother used to take Ruth and me to the dressmaker, Frau Dichter, in Berlin. We spent hours selecting just the right fabrics, then we'd return a few weeks later for a fitting. Frau Dichter, with pins in her mouth, made us walk back and forth and turn slowly while she pinned and repinned, until everything was perfect.

I wished I were like Mama, not caring about clothes and cosmetics. But I did care! I wanted my hair to shine, my legs to look sleek in silk stockings and high-heeled shoes. I studied movie magazines to see how the stars wore their makeup. With my first paycheck I went to the drugstore and bought myself a lipstick. It came in a beautiful gold case, and it cost seventy-nine cents. Ruth was astounded.

''You spent seventy-nine cents for a lipstick? Are you crazy? You could get one for fourteen cents!''

"Not like this," I said warmly. "Look at the color! The gold case is so gorgeous."

"You had to work over two hours for that!" Ruth exclaimed.

"It was worth it."

For once, I thought, I owned the best of something, not the cheapest.

Will Alexander came over to our house on Sundays. To wash his car, he said.

Papa threw up his hands, laughing. "Here he has to wash the car? At home he has no water?"

"Silly," Mother said, smiling in that special way she had when it came to romance, "he is coming to see Ruth, and you know it."

"Boys are always coming to see Ruth!" he exclaimed. "I can hardly get in the door. It's like having a dog in heat."

"Hush, Arthur, what a thing to say!"

"Well, well, they tell me when you have three daughters, and each one more beautiful than the next . . ."

"Lisa and Annie have plenty of time for such things," Mama said. "Stop putting ideas into their heads."

But of course, Papa was putting nothing into my head that wasn't already there. Sheila, Louise, Janine, and I talked about boys constantly, pored over the pictures of men in movie magazines, pinned them up on our walls, and plotted how to make various boys like us. I was still working on Will Alexander.

Some Sundays I made it my business to be outside. This day I was playing ball with Annie. She had a good arm; she was practicing to be on the softball team.

I threw her a high fly. Annie had gotten an old mitt

from the Goodwill store, and now she ran, then leaped for the ball, catching it neatly in the mitt.

I heard applause. "Great catch!"

I turned, feigning surprise, though of course I had been watching for Will's car from the corner of my eye. "Oh, Will," I said nonchalantly.

"Oh, hi, Will," Annie mimicked me. She knew exactly why I'd agreed to play with her.

"What's going on?" Will asked.

"Ruth's washing her hair," I told him, with that catching feeling in my throat.

Will smiled. "Girls sure love to wash their hair, don't they?"

"The way boys love to wash their cars, I guess."

Will laughed. "Want to help me wash it?"

"Sure."

We turned on the hose, made a bucket of suds.

"How many cylinders have you got in the engine?" I asked, dipping in my rag, bringing it up over the hood.

"Why—six," Will answered, surprised. "It's got plenty of power."

"I guess she'd do up to seventy out on the flat," I said. "Have you ever tried it?"

"Oh, sure." He grinned. "Once I took her up to eighty-five, out in the desert near Palm Springs. I've never told anybody, though. My dad would scalp me."

"I won't tell anyone."

"Not even your sister?"

"Ruth and I don't talk all that much," I said. Any feelings of disloyalty to Ruth were quickly overcome by the greater feeling of sharing something with Will. I wanted him to confide in me.

"Is Ruth—uh—is she seeing a lot of other guys?"

"Lots of guys come over," I said. "To see us," I added.

"I hear you might enter the talent show."

"I've been thinking of it."

"Ruth says you're a sensational dancer."

Now I really felt like a rat.

Annie interrupted. "Can I polish the chrome, Will?"

"Sure, kid. Thanks. Some people think we should disband the club altogether," Will said.

"How come?" I felt elated. Here he was, standing and talking to me, his face serious, eyes looking straight into mine. It didn't matter what we said—the fact that we were talking was enough.

"Well, we're like the Japs, you know. Enemy aliens. A lot of people think all the Germans ought to be rounded up, too. Kept in camps somewhere until the war's over. So some of the members think we should disband the club. They think it might attract too much attention to us, and then . . ."

"You mean—they'd put us in concentration camps? Here?"

Will shook his head, frowning. "Not like those camps in Germany and Poland," he said. His voice had dropped to a whisper. "There, they kill people. You've heard."

"Yes." I was whispering, too.

"Americans don't do things like that. They're just keeping the Japs segregated. Still, I wouldn't want to have to live in a camp."

I shuddered.

Ruth appeared. "Hi, Will." She smiled at him.

Will immediately turned from me and went to her. "Hi, gorgeous," he said.

Chapter 13

I PRACTICED MY DANCE in the gym early each morning and again in the afternoon, in preparation for the club talent contest. I could hear the music in my mind. It never occurred to me to ask Madame K. whether I could play the actual record.

One early morning as I finished a turn, there stood Madame K. braced in the doorway.

"Not a bad routine," she said. "You could add a few dips at the end, and how about the beginning . . ." She showed me a few steps, moving with remarkable grace.

"That would be better," I conceded.

"What about music?"

"I have music at home. A record. 'The Glow Worm.'"

"Ah, yes." The teacher began to hum a few bars, tapping her bamboo cane, waving her hand for me to dance.

I danced. She sang, speeding up the tempo, pulling in my performance with the tapping of her cane, the sweep of her hand. . . . "Higher, higher, yes, yes, eyes ahead! Leg straight! Point that toe!"

The pure exhilaration of performing came over me as I ended in a deep bow.

"Tomorrow, bring the record," the teacher ordered. "Then we can do it properly. Your *tour jeté* is sloppy, and you are letting your stomach go out. Quite disgraceful! When are you performing your dance for this—what group is it?"

"The German Jewish Club," I said, without blinking an eye. It was a matter of principle with me to tell her this. "The contest is in two weeks."

"You have a great deal of work to do then, if you intend to win. And," she added, her chin high, "I am not accustomed to coaching losers, do you understand?"

"Yes, Madame."

"Do you have a costume?"

"I'm making one," I said. Papa had gotten me a yard and a half of pale blue tulle. Very carefully I was making a tutu, planning to buy blue tights and a leotard to go with it. I would make a tulle crown for my hair. Papa was so proud of my sewing! "Chip from the old timer!" he called me, mixing his slang.

One day, while I was in my room sewing, I heard Papa shout. "Girls! Girls!"

I finished the seam and ran out to the living room, where Papa stood, calling again, holding a violin case.

Ruth stood before him, frozen, her face set in an expression I don't think I'd ever seen before. Amazement. Longing. Resentment. Anger. All these feelings seemed locked into that frozen look and Papa—poor Papa, in his excitement he didn't even notice.

"What is it?" I said, though of course I could see what
it was.

Papa gazed at Ruth. "It's a violin," he said. "I went
past a pawn shop today, and in the window . . . it's not
the best violin in the world," he said. "A Stradivarius it
isn't. But it was there in the window, and I had never
seen it before, so I thought . . . go in, I thought. So I
went in. I didn't want to buy it if someone was coming
back for it, you know. I mean, a poor musician who had
to pawn his violin—it would be terrible for him to lose
it. But the man in the pawn shop told me it had belonged
to his uncle, who died. And so I thought . . . of course,
Ruth, I thought of you."

Mother had told Papa, of course, what had happened
to Ruth's violin, how at the border when we were leaving
Germany the Nazis took it away from her. It was an old
memory, but I still feit that terrible pain, a twisting feeling
in the stomach, hatred mixed with fear, and shock at Ruth's
loss. Ruth had never mentioned the violin again. She had
sealed herself away from music, digging deep into her studies and her reading.

Now she stared at Papa, while he said, "Open it, Ruth."

Ruth shook her head.

"Well, then I'll open it," Papa said, unsnapping the
fasteners. The case was old, lined with dark-blue velvet,
and the violin inside had certainly seen better days. It was
scratched and dull, the bow was a little ragged. But Papa
lifted it out and held it up like a treasure.

"Here! It's for you!" Papa cried joyfully, and he stepped
toward Ruth, the violin extended. "Take it, my dear, it's
yours!"

I heard a gasp. I looked at Ruth. She was shaking her
head, her hands clenched together under her chin.

"What's the matter, Ruth?"

Still she shook her head. "No," she whispered at last, a hoarse croak. "No, Papa. Don't make me. Please."

"But what's the matter with you, child? I thought . . . I thought you'd be happy. I only wanted to make you . . . *happy.*"

"I'm sorry, Papa," Ruth whispered, still in that strange, cracked tone. "I can't play anymore. I just can't."

I trembled, dimly aware that something more was happening here, something Ruth could not explain in words. Ruth's loss had been too shattering; she could not try to undo the past.

But Papa smiled and said merrily, "Nonsense, Ruth, of course you can. Once you have played the violin, you never forget. Oh, of course one must practice again, because the fingers grow stiff from disuse—but the heart? Never!"

So saying, Papa placed the violin under his chin, for he had played as a boy, as had all his brothers. He slid the bow across the strings a few times, and I saw the shiver moving across Ruth's back, as if that bow were cutting into her flesh, cutting away the forgetfulness she had at last achieved.

Papa plucked the strings into tune, then whipped out a song, a gay polka, stamping one foot in rhythm, swinging from that into one of the German *lieder*. By then Annie had emerged, and she stood in the doorway listening, entranced.

"And you must remember this one," Papa said, failing to notice, perhaps, that Ruth had slipped away and only Annie and I remained to listen.

"This was always my favorite," he murmured. With his eyes closed and the violin resting gently under his chin, Papa lifted his arm once more and began to play an old

German song we all knew, *"Heimat,"* which means
"Homeland."

Will continued to come over to wash his car regularly.
"Where's Ruth?" he asked.

"I don't know," I said. "Maybe at her friend Elinor's.
They study together sometimes."

He gave a laugh. "So, how about you?" he asked. He
glanced about, jiggled his keys. "Are you busy?"

"Busy? I—no. I guess . . ."

"Want to go for a ride?"

"I'd love it!"

I ran in to tell Mother. "Please let me go," I said. My
voice was very low. I did not want Will to hear.

"Don't let him drive too fast," Mother said, with a
long look at me. For a moment I thought she'd say something
about Ruth, about sisters being in competition. But she
only added, "Take a sweater in case it gets cool."

"Oh, thank you, Mama!" I gave her a hug.

"Where do you want to go?" Will asked.

"Hollywood," I instantly replied.

We drove. I told Will about school, especially about
the dancing class. Madame K. had put me in the front
row, and she often said, "Watch Lisa, girls. Lisa Platt
knows how to do it!"

"Do you want to dance professionally?" Will asked.

"More than anything in the world."

"Then do it," he said.

"It takes a lot of money for lessons," I said.

"You can earn the money."

"I do work," I said. "I sew for my father, and on
Saturdays I work at the bakery."

"Great," Will said. "It's good to keep busy." He smiled. "I remember in Germany, we never worked on Saturdays. Nobody did. My grandparents were very religious. Very strict."

"What did you do, then?" I asked.

"Oh, it was wonderful. We went for long walks to the park; we listened to music."

"You didn't pray?" My tone was light, almost joking.

"Music is sort of like praying, isn't it?"

I felt a lump in my throat. I loved him! He was so sensitive, so understanding, so mature.

"I took out a savings account at Bank of America," I said with pride. "I've got thirty-five dollars in it."

"That's great," Will said. "All the extra money I have goes into this car. Of course, I'll have that problem solved for me very soon, by Uncle Sam. We'll be leaving before too long."

"Leaving?" I felt as if I'd been knocked down flat. "Where are you going?"

"Didn't Ruth tell you?" He shook his head. "It figures," he said, almost to himself. "A bunch of us are going over together."

"Over? Where? What do you mean?"

"We joined up. I'm going to be a soldier!"

"Don't you have to be an American citizen to be in the army?"

"No. We have to be cleared and found loyal. That we are. We want overseas duty. We want to go over there and show them! Gary, Tony, Richard, and I all signed up together. We'll be in the same unit."

"You—you'll go to Germany? To fight?" I thought of the people I knew there, the people I'd left behind. For the first time, I began to imagine what it might be like to live with fighting in the streets, houses being shattered. Until now, the newsreels seemed just like so many pictures, like stories.

"Some of my American friends can't understand," Will said. "They say, 'How can you fight against your own countrymen?' Well, they're not my countrymen anymore. They booted us out! They wanted to kill us all! I don't understand how any Jew would ever want to live in Germany again."

He was so passionate, so handsome! Of course, I understood.

"So—when will you leave?" I could hardly breathe.

"I'm not sure. They'll let us know. Maybe a few weeks, maybe a month or two."

We drove along Hollywood Boulevard with its specialty shops, by the USO, where soldiers and sailors stood outside, milling about. There was a row of glittering movie theaters, and then the star walk, where brass stars were imbedded into the sidewalk, each inscribed with a famous actor's name.

"Wouldn't you love to be famous?" I said.

"I guess," Will said. "Mostly, I just want to get this war over with. We're all sort of in limbo, you know?" He stood close to me. I could see our faces reflected in the store window. He put his hand on my back, then around my shoulder. "We can't really make any plans. We can't even think about a career until—until we get this war over with."

"I know," I murmured.

He said, "When we leave, would you come to the station to see us off?"

My heart leaped crazily. I nodded, too happy to speak.

"You and Ruth," he added.

"Me and Ruth?" I seemed to be hearing echoes.

"Charlotta's coming down. There'll be a lot of guys. Everyone will have someone to see him off."

"Did you ask Ruth?"

He shrugged. "You know Ruth. She said she didn't know."

"So now you're asking me."

"What's wrong with that?" he exclaimed, suddenly defensive, almost harsh. "If you don't want to," he said, "it's all right."

Oh, I wanted to. Didn't he know it? Couldn't he tell?

"Of course we'll come," I said.

He moved aside. "Who's this guy Ruth's going with?"

"What guy?" My heart was leaping wildly. I felt as though I were being tossed about on the ocean.

"You mean she isn't going with that guy?"

"I don't know what you're talking about. Will, if you want to know about Ruth, why don't you talk to her? Why are you always . . ."

"I'm sorry. I'm sorry." Quickly he came to me, put his arm around me and then, turning, he kissed me. Not on the mouth, as I had supposed, not at all the way I had imagined his first kiss. He brushed my lips quickly, almost the way he'd kiss his sister.

"Come on," he said. "I'll get us an ice-cream cone."

The night of the talent show arrived and I won!

What is there to say when one is the winner? Everyone knows that feeling at some time or other. To be the top. To be the best. To receive the applause, the smiles, kisses, bouquets, and then the predictions of still grander things to come.

"She will be a movie star one day, Margo, wait and see."

"So graceful, so lovely. She reminds me a little of Sonja Henie, don't you think?"

"Well, well, Arthur, how does it feel to be the father of three such beautiful and talented girls?"

Suddenly, it was my glory that spread to the rest of the family. The man pinched Annie's cheek. "Aren't you proud of your sister?"

Annie had made a terrible fuss about coming; she hated to be "with all those Germans," she said. Now she was smiling.

"She's the best dancer I've ever seen," Annie said.

"Do you dance, too, Annie?"

"No. I'm as awkward as an elephant child." That sent the old folks into peals of laughter as they discussed among themselves who was the prettiest of us three, who the cleverest, who the most talented.

They always talked that way. Before, it had bothered me. Tonight, I ate it up.

Will came up to me, walking with Ruth and several of the other young people. "Congratulations," he said. "You are a real professional."

"Congratulations, Lisa," Ruth echoed. "You were marvelous."

"A bunch of us are going out for ice cream," Will said, motioning to the group of fellows and girls. "Want to come with us?"

I tried not to show my excitement, tossed my head, and said, "Sure, why not?"

It was the best night of my life. Seven of us piled into Will's car. Ruth sat beside him in front, and then Gary, while I sat in back with Charlotta, Tony, and Richard. I had never imagined that just riding in a car could be an adventure. We sang. We laughed.

We stopped at a drive-in, but decided to go inside instead of eating in the car, for we wanted to hear the juke-box.

Inside, the place glittered with bright lights, shiny table-tops, sleek counters. The jukebox gave off its music along with a rainbow of colors, twirling and swirling from red to green to yellow to blue.

We ordered hot-fudge sundaes. "No fudge," said the waitress, "and no walnuts."

"What?" we exclaimed. "How come? How do you make a hot-fudge sundae without fudge?"

The girl shrugged, tapping her foot. "There's a war on," she said.

"We're winning the war with hot fudge and walnuts!" I cried happily, lifting my water glass in a toast. "Here's a cheer!"

"Hurrah!" said the boys, clapping their hands upon the table.

"I'll have a strawberry sundae with butterscotch topping." I decided.

"Fabulous!" Gary agreed. "Make that two."

"Two for him and one for me," said I.

Everyone laughed.

"Make that three," said Will. "Three for me, two for him, one for her."

We were laughing so hard that someone spilled a glass of water.

"Tony, can I have a hamburger?" Charlotta asked, making doe eyes at him.

"You can have anything you want, sweetheart," Tony said with a grin. "Next week I'm going to meet a guy who has a connection with nylon stockings. I'll get you a pair.''

"Oh, Tony, you're so wonderful!" Charlotta shouted out. "How will I live without you?"

Suddenly things settled down. A new tune came on the jukebox. In the tiny space at the back of the diner, between the last row of booths and the wall, two couples were dancing.

Will took Ruth's hand. "Want to dance?"

"I'd love to."

The two of them left; I could see them dancing. He held her very close. His face was half-hidden in her hair.

I danced with Gary and then with Richard, wishing desperately for Will to ask me. But he didn't. Too soon it was time to leave. We all had to be off the streets by ten-thirty.

Ruth and I went into the house. We stood in the darkened living room. "Lisa," she whispered, "do you like Will?"

"Yes," I admitted.

"You can have him," she whispered back.

"How can you talk about him like that?" I exclaimed. "He's not yours to take or give away, like some old handkerchief."

"I see the way you look at him," she said. "Actually, I always thought he was more your type than mine."

I remembered what Will had said, about Ruth going with someone else.

"Ruth, is there something you haven't told me? I thought we always shared our secrets."

Suddenly Ruth burst into tears.

"What is it? What is it?" I cried, alarmed.

"Come into my bedroom. I'm dying to tell you. Oh, Lisa, I'm in love."

Chapter 14

WE SAT DOWN on Ruth's bed. Ruth's little room was cool and clean; the screened windows were shadowed with oleander branches. We could smell the muted scent of the blossoms. Ruth had put on the little light beside her bed. She was so pretty there in that light, wearing a pink blouse with a little lace collar, her dark eyes shining and her lips parted as she said again, "I'm in love, Lisa. This time it's real."

"Tell me," I breathed, staring at her. "Who is he? Where did you meet him? Why haven't you told me?"

"Oh, Lisa!" Ruth sighed. "His name is Peter. Peter Ross. He is—he is the most . . . Well, I met him at the canteen."

"When? Why didn't you tell me? Have you told Will? Is that what he meant when he said . . ."

"Hold on!" Ruth laughed slightly. "I guess Will sort of suspected. But there was nothing to tell. Not at first.

And then . . . what could I tell you? That I was in love
with a pilot who . . . ?''

"A pilot!"

"His home is in Michigan. He's been stationed out here
for the last three months. I met him exactly ten weeks
ago. I—he wants me to marry him, Lisa.''

I felt a shiver along my spine; my hair seemed to rise
on the back of my neck.

"Marry?'' I could hardly get the word out.

"Not right away, of course,'' Ruth said quickly.' "But
in a while—maybe when he comes back on furlough, maybe
in a year or two. Oh, Lisa, he's so wonderful!'' Ruth
took my arm, gave it a squeeze. "Let me tell you all
about him.''

"Yes, yes!'' I cried. I felt like laughing and weeping
both at the same time, suddenly drawn into this drama
that involved not some stranger on a movie screen, but
Ruth, my own sister, who in some ways was the closest
person to me in the world.

"Well,'' she began, looking mysterious, "I was serving
coffee and doughnuts to all the boys when I noticed this
guy was just standing there watching me, not saying anything, not asking for anything. I sort of caught a look at
him, you know? Out of the corner of my eye. And something
about him—I felt so . . . Well, I tried not to look at him,
but I felt him staring. So I said, 'Aren't you going to
have anything?' and he said, 'What are you offering me?'
kind of cocky, you know, so I didn't crack a smile, and I
said, 'Coffee and doughnuts, like all the other boys.' So
he said, 'But I'm not like all the other boys.' So—well,
we started to talk. He kept drinking coffee and eating doughnuts.'' Ruth giggled. "Later he told me he'd never had

so much coffee in his entire life. He couldn't get to sleep all night. And he never wants to look another doughnut in the face again. I think he had seven of them."

I laughed. "How old is he?" I asked.

"Twenty-three."

"Twenty-three!"

"He has light brown hair. Wavy hair. Brown eyes. He sort of has dimples, and he's six feet tall. When he puts his arms around me, I just . . ."

"When did he put his arms around you?"

"We're not supposed to date the boys we meet at the canteen, you know," Ruth said. She stood up, walked a few steps, sat down again. "But he'd come and wait for me, and we'd walk around the block."

"Didn't Mother see?"

"No! She was always in the building with the blood donors. The canteen is outside on the corner. So we'd walk. Then he'd put his arm around me. It was . . . I've never felt like this in my life, Lisa. It's like being completely new. Reborn. Everything's changed. And suddenly I—I understand things."

"What things?" I breathed.

"Like wanting to do everything for someone. Wanting to be with them more than anything. Like sex."

The word seemed to burn a path between us.

"What about it?" I said, my voice hoarse.

"When he kisses me . . ."

"Is that all you've done?"

"Lisa! That's not the point."

"What do you do with Peter?" I knew Ruth would not tell me everything; she liked privacy.

"Lisa, when he kisses me, I forget everything else. I've

never really cared about that sort of thing before. The boys always want to neck, want to touch . . . I always pushed them away. It was always like a contest. . . .''

"With Will, too?''

She brushed me aside. "All of them—all alike, and I hated it! But when Peter kisses me, I sort of want to— gee, I guess I just sort of—melt.''

I nodded. I wanted that, too! I wanted someone to kiss me and hold me, and I wanted to feel those feelings. Especially, I wanted Will.

"I'm happy for you,'' I whispered.

"Thank you, Lisa.''

"Does Mother know?''

"I think she suspects something. But I haven't talked to her about him. And she hasn't noticed—this.'' Ruth pulled open the first button of her blouse. There on a gold chain hung a ring, a man's gold ring.

"We're engaged to be engaged,'' Ruth whispered.

"Oh, my God!'' I cried.

"So I'm going to see him Saturday night. It'll be our first whole evening together. Will said the kids are all going to the movies together. He means you, too. But I'm not going to go. Don't you see? I can't.''

"What'll you tell Will? What'll you tell Mother?''

Ruth shrugged. "You can tell Will anything you want. I have to do this, Lisa. I don't care what Mother says. I'm not a child anymore.''

I went to my room and sat in the darkness, then lit the candle and wrote in my diary:

January 9, 1943. Ruth is in love with Peter Ross, a pilot. How odd it seems for her to be in love with someone

I don't even know. Someday we will all get married, and we might not even live in the same city! It seems impossible to believe. I would never want to live far from Annie and Ruth. How do sisters move away from each other without dying of loneliness?

The boys are all leaving. Going to war. When I was walking to school yesterday I passed a large field, and suddenly I had the strangest thought! We learned about the battle of Flanders Field in World War One at school, and we saw a picture of it, with trees and rocks. And I realized, a battlefield is just like any other place! It can be a street in front of somebody's house, or a road leading to somebody's farm, or even a school yard. No place is ever meant as a battlefield. It just gets to be one because soldiers fight there. And it was the strangest feeling to be looking at those trees and to realize that in Germany and France and all those other countries, men are shooting right where other people are living, and houses are getting wrecked.

Nobody has ever really kissed me. I wonder what it's like? I know people do it with their mouth, open. Janine told me all about a French kiss she got. It sounds so intimate! I would really have to be crazy about a boy before I'd let him put his tongue in my mouth. But with all the boys leaving and going to war, I guess there won't be anybody left to kiss. Maybe, if the war keeps on much longer, there won't be anybody left to marry, and we'll all be old maids.

A few days after I learned Ruth was in love, Janine, Louise, five other girls, and I were invited to Sheila's house. Three or four of them had met together before, with the idea to start a club. There were several social clubs at school. Members wore club sweaters and club pins; they ate lunch together, had teas and dances, and rushed around, always looking as if they had something important and exciting to do.

Janine and I talked about it a great deal. We'd been invited to join, though we weren't exactly like the other girls. We were both foreigners. Our families were different. Our homes were plain, especially compared to Sheila's and Louise's. And yet they wanted us, were willing to include us in the group.

Sheila's mother had prepared beautiful refreshments for our meeting. A large silver tray stood on the highly polished coffee table, filled with cookies and cake.

I noticed everything: the soft blue carpet, the rounded sofa, the fine china, golden-edged plates with small blue flowers, the teapot with matching cream-and-sugar servers, and a cut-glass plate upon which were arranged fre. slices of lemon.

Louise acted as the "temporary" president, using a small ashtray to tap us into silence. We all knew she would be the actual president of the new club. I watched her admiringly; she knew exactly what to do.

"The meeting will please come to order," she said firmly, but with a smile at everyone. "Now, we'll need to think of a good name for our club, something that sounds cultured and sophisticated, but not stuffy. We have several suggestions, and we can discuss them and then take a vote."

We heard the choices: Acadians, Olympianas, Elysians. We unanimously chose the last. Elysium, as Louise explained, was a mythical place of perfect peace and happiness.

I repeated the name to myself, already filled with joy.

"We'll have an opening tea," Louise suggested. "We

can have it at my house, out in the garden. I'll ask my mother if we can get Cora to serve. We can buy petits fours, those tiny ones from the French bakery, and little cream puffs. . . ."

"And I'll ask Mom if we can use her tea service," Sheila put in.

"We'll have to have invitations engraved," suggested another girl. "My mother knows where to get them made."

They went on and on, and I was set to dreaming of the gorgeous affairs I'd attend, wearing gorgeous clothes, being a part of this elegant club, living the kind of life I'd always known I was destined for. We'd have dances at a country club; we'd hire a name band, have engraved bids. . . . All these girls had lived in a world where such things were commonplace. How much I'd learn from being with them! I watched them as they talked, watched how they ate, how they drank their tea, held their napkins. One reached over to a side table, took a cigarette from the box, and carefully lit it.

I watched the others, to see what impression this made.

"Sarah!" cried one of them. "I didn't know you smoked, you wicked old thing!"

"Well, there's a lot you don't know about me, I guess," replied Sarah, exhaling through rounded lips.

They all laughed, and another girl lit up, too, and then it was back to business.

Janine and I took the bus toward home, dazzled and amazed at it all. "It will cost a fortune to be in that club, I guess," said Janine. "But it will be worth it."

"Oh, the fun, the fun," I murmured. I tried not to think of the fortune. I had money saved, after all, and I intended to go on working. I'd work my fingers to the bone just to be an Elysian.

Chapter 15

As if to indicate that prosperity was really coming into our lives, Papa bought a car. He announced it late one afternoon with several blasts of a husky horn.

Annie came screaming to get me.

"Come outside, Lisa! Hurry! You won't believe it."

There in our driveway stood a hulking, sputtering, black Chevrolet at least eight years old, and behind the wheel, smoking nonchalantly, sat Papa. That night Papa was jubilant. Since he needed the car for his business, Papa had also been given a "C" ration sticker.

"No more buses! I can put all my samples in the trunk, and no more carrying them on my back. Now," he declared, "I feel like a prince."

"I'm glad you are happy, Arthur," Mother said.

Looking back, we were all too busy with our own affairs, I suppose, to notice that Mother was not herself. It took a jolt to show us; we were all blind, all involved in our own pursuits—Ruth with Peter, Annie with her softball

team, Papa with his car, and I with my friends and, especially, my dancing. Madame Klausenstock had announced
that there would be a large Liberty Bond drive at the Shrine
Auditorium, with various groups of young people performing. All the proceeds from tickets and bond sales would
go to the war effort. Madame Klausenstock was choosing
twelve of us to perform.

"It is your duty, if you are chosen," the teacher barked
out, "to devote yourself faithfully to the program. I shall
expect from every girl one hundred percent partici-
pation. That means absolute promptness at rehearsals, no
absences whatsoever, and perfect attention to every as-
pect of the body which contributes to the success of the
dance."

A few girls snickered. Most of us stood ramrod straight,
eyes ahead, realizing that if we were chosen, nothing about
our person would remain sacred. Madame would tell us
what to eat, what to wear, when to sleep, how to breathe.
We would, for the duration, belong to her. But it would
be worth the price.

"Any of you who imagines that such a regimen is too
difficult, speak out at the beginning. Because anyone failing
to cooperate, anyone who drops out of the group for any
reason whatsoever, receives an F in the class and, I promise
you, will never again dance in any program with which I
am associated."

All week, Madame would devote herself to choosing.
Next week, she promised, a list of the chosen would be
posted on the gymnasium door.

"Of course you'll be on it," Sheila said encouragingly.
"You're one of the best dancers she has."

"There could be producers in the audience," Louise
said. "You could be discovered."

"It's like being in a real professional show," Janine added.

I didn't dare tell them how much I wanted it. I didn't even dare tell myself. The word *professional,* when it was applied to the dance, always filled me with awe. To dance for a living? How could anything be more wonderful?

I rushed home, hoping that Papa would be there. But the garage door was shut. He was still downtown. I went into Ruth's room. It was, as usual, immaculate, her extra blanket folded neatly on the foot of her bed, books straight in rows, clothes hung neatly in her small closet, which had no door, but a drawstring cotton curtain.

I knew she was meeting Peter most afternoons. He was being shipped out soon. Being a pilot sounded romantic. It was also dangerous. He would be sent on bombing missions overseas.

I stood in Ruth's room for several minutes. The scent of Ruth, her presence, her longing was here in this room. "I love him!" she had told me again just last night. "He's leaving next week, Lisa. He wants me to . . ."

Just then Papa had called us for something. The moment was lost.

I went into the kitchen. It was as Mother had left it this morning, oatmeal pot soaking in the sink, clean dishes in the drainer. Crumbs on the floor. I reached for the broom.

I heard an indefinite sound—muffled, anguished.

Tiptoeing, I went down the hall. Mother's bedroom door was shut. Carefully I opened it.

There she lay, on her side, knees drawn up. Her hair lay loosely around her, the gray strands seeming to clutch at the pillow, the way her hands clutched at her stomach.

"Mama!" I rushed to the bed, knelt there, put my hand

on her forehead. It was hot and damp. She looked at me, her eyes very dark, the pupils large, and as she breathed I felt the short gasps against my cheek, smelled her sharp breath, realized that she was in terrible pain.

"What is it? What is it?"

She shook her head, rolling it from side to side across the pillow.

"Did you come home from work? Were you ill? Is that why you came home?"

"I—left. I felt . . . unwell." She shook her head. "When I came home the letter was here. It was already here." And then she began to cry.

I had seen my mother cry before. But not like this.

This was a different cry; into a terrible void her tears fell, as if they were endless. Three words, three sounds separated themselves from her tears, and I realized it was these that I had heard in the kitchen, the same three sounds repeated in different combinations, but with the same agony—"Why? Oh, God. Oh, God, why? Why? Why?"

She spoke in German. *"Warum? Ach Gott, warum?"* The words resounded, lingered, like definite shapes haunting the room.

"What letter?" I asked.

She did not answer.

"Where does it hurt?"

"I threw up," Mother said. I was astonished. I had never known that to happen to Mother before.

I glanced about, saw the envelope on the bureau, official looking, with the words RED CROSS printed in the corner.

"Red Cross?" I said half-aloud. I supposed it had something to do with Mother's volunteer work. Then I looked

again. It was postmarked from New York, and the return
address read OFFICE OF MISSING PERSONS.

As if I had been here earlier in the day, I knew exactly
how my mother's hand must have trembled, how her head
throbbed and her body and mind steeled itself for this moment. I saw by the careful cut across the top of the envelope
how slowly and carefully she had taken a sharp knife and
made one long, single slit, the way a surgeon makes his
swift but precise incision in living flesh. I imagined her
slim fingers reaching into the envelope, as mine did now,
to take out the single sheet of paper, crisply folded, formally
and perfectly typed:

> *Dear Mrs. Platt:*
>
> *After exhaustive inquiries into the case of your
> mother, Lucille Weiss, née Grossman, of Berlin,
> Germany, it is our duty to inform you that reliable
> sources state that she was deported from her
> home to the camp at Auschwitz, sometime in
> January 1943. While the particular details of
> your mother's situation are not known to us,
> we can tell you only that generally in these cases
> there is nothing more that can be done.*
>
> *Our efforts on behalf of family reunification
> will continue and if we can again be of service
> to you, do not hesitate to call on us.*

Only one word in that letter was significant. *Auschwitz.*
Auschwitz was one of the death camps we had heard
about. Grandmother was dead, had been dead for months
while we lived out our lives here in California.

Grandmother. Auschwitz. Dead.

Now, I could not really remember her face. I remembered

her coat, a dark coat with a fur collar, and the little hat she usually wore when she came over to our apartment in Berlin, bringing with her a box of pastries. I would hear her and Mama talking and talking. A hundred times I saw them taking leave, my mother bending to kiss her mother's cheek, to say, *"Gruss Gott,"* "Go with God."

I felt as if I had stood there for hours. Actually, the hand of the clock jumped but a minute ahead. My mother still lay there on her side, her eyes closed now, hands clutched under her chin.

I tiptoed to her side. I felt ashamed, somehow.

"I'll call Papa," I said at last.

Mother did not answer. I saw that her face was streaked with sweat, and her eyes were glazed. I realized then that it was not only the letter, but something else added to it, that had laid her onto this bed.

I ran lightly to the living room. At that moment Annie came home, flinging down her books. "Mother's sick," I said. "Make some tea and take it to her. Feed her small spoonfuls. I'm going to call Papa."

Annie instantly obeyed.

I called the factory; the number was penciled on the wall beside the telephone. I remembered how Mother had scolded Papa for writing on the wall. Now I was glad he did.

Papa came to the telephone, already on edge; they had told him, "Arthur, it's your daughter."

"What's wrong?"

"Mother's sick. It's bad, Papa. Come home."

Less than fifteen minutes later he was there. He rushed into the bedroom, where Annie and I sat, holding Mother's hands.

He pointed to the door.

Annie and I hurried out.

Then we heard them.

"Gott! Ach Gott, warum? Warum?"

Why? Why? Why?

"Margo, oh Margo, my darling, beloved, oh, Margo."

Five minutes passed. Ten. Then Papa rushed out, went to the telephone, made a brief call to his friend, Mr. Miles. "Harry! I need a doctor. The best doctor you know. My wife . . ."

When Ruth came home we told her everything. She sat down with Annie and me in the living room, the three of us side by side on the sofa, not a word spoken between us. Sometimes there is just nothing to say.

Once, Papa came out to tell us, "The doctor is coming."

"What's the matter, Papa? What's wrong with Mother?"

"She's a very sick woman."

"From the letter?"

"We'll see."

The doctor came a few minutes later, Dr. Belzac, a European who, we later discovered, spoke several languages, including German. Every movement of his was serious and determined; he walked in, sized us up with a glance, gave us a brief nod, and went directly to Mother's room.

When he emerged, we held a conference in the living room, we three keeping silent, of course, with Papa questioning.

"Is it a nervous condition? Is it a breakdown? In Switzerland, when she was alone with the girls, she had . . ."

"Your wife has been suffering for many months, Mr. Platt," Dr. Belzac said. "But she's going to be all right. The poor woman got it into her head that she had cancer of the stomach."

"Cancer!" Ruth gasped.

Dr. Belzac held up his hand. "It's not cancer. I believe it's her gallbladder. We must remove the gallbladder; it is severely diseased. We should operate as soon as possible."

Papa said, "Doctor, she will not want an operation. I know my wife. She is very afraid of operations."

I had ghastly visions of surgery; I had seen only a few photographs in magazines, of doctors masked and gowned, and strange instruments being used, and I'd heard of anesthetics.

"We have no choice, Mr. Platt," the doctor said. "Because of your wife's emotional state, she has let this thing go on much too long. She should have come to me long ago, with those terrible pains. . . ."

"I would have brought her to you!" my father cried. "Why didn't she tell me? I never knew."

"She felt she was suffering from an incurable disease. Mr. Platt, these things are complicated, and I'm not a psychiatrist. But you have told me about the letter, and what happened to your wife's mother. I think your wife knew, even before the letter came. She had heard nothing from her mother in many months. She reads the newspapers and knows what is going on. Your wife had to know beforehand that her mother would not survive the Nazi's annihilation plan."

"And this is why she got sick?"

"Ah, my friend, guilt and grief cause more sickness than anything else in the world. Who can tell exactly what goes on in the human heart, and in the mind? Cancer—maybe your poor wife saw cancer as the punishment for her failure to save her mama. So when she began having the pains, she assumed the worst. How could she know it was her gallbladder? And today, of all days . . ."—he

threw up his hands—"early this morning she took a dose
of castor oil. Oil is the worst thing for someone with a
gallbladder condition."

He looked at all of us with a strange smile, shaking his
head, a gesture of weariness and yet of warmth. He had a
kind face, deep-set dark eyes over heavy brows, a large
nose, a mouth expressive, quick to smile, quick to turn
down in sympathy.

"Listen, my friend, let's solve the immediate problem
first. We should operate as soon as possible."

"Tomorrow?" Papa asked.

"I can call and see if we can get the operating room
tomorrow. It is not wise to wait."

Papa wiped his forehead with his handkerchief. "What
costs such an operation?"

"Don't worry about that now," said Dr. Belzac. "We'll
work out whatever you can afford."

Ruth, Annie, and I walked over to the delicatessen and
bought some food for supper. We sat in the breakfast nook,
talking for hours.

We realized, I think, that we had each become an island,
absorbed and isolated by our own needs and desires. That
night was the longest ever; suddenly the whole world was
locked into these small rooms, and the five of us were
once again connected, close.

That night I wrote in my diary.

*March 5, 1943. Grandmother is dead. Mother is very
sick. I wish I had been better to her, instead of just thinking
about Will and the Elysians all the time. I've been lying
to her, too. Maybe not lying directly, but letting her think
Ruth was with Will and me and the others, when I knew*

she was really sneaking out with Peter. Is God punishing me? All I've been thinking about is doing things with Will. When I see him, I hardly say anything, I get so nervous. So of course he must think I'm a real jerk.

See? Here Mother is sick and Grandmother is dead, and I still just write about Will—I guess I must be one of the most selfish people in the world. Annie made Mother the sweetest little card tonight. She painted it herself. Tomorrow I'll clean the whole house for Mother, and I'll make her some custard. When the war is over, if Mother goes back to Germany to see her mama's grave, she'll never find it. We'll never know where Grandmother was buried. That's what happens in a war. I never thought of things like this before. I and the other girls have been knitting socks and squares for afghans, to send to the soldiers. I wonder whether the girlfriends and wives of Nazis are doing the same. I don't care! I hate them!

Chapter 16

THE NEXT DAY Mama was taken by ambulance to the hospital for the operation.

Ruth and I rode with Mother in the ambulance. Papa took Annie in the car to meet us there. Mother had been given a sedative. She was pale, but no longer crying. In fact, she was annoyed.

"Imagine, taking me in an ambulance! What a lot of fuss over nothing!"

But she looked worn-out as she lay on the white sheets. She reached out, took Ruth's hand. "Ruth," she whispered, "when are you going to see your young man again?"

Instantly Ruth flushed and bit her lip. "What young man?"

Mother smiled slightly. "I don't know his name. The handsome one, fair-haired. From the canteen."

"Mama, how did you know?"

"I'm your mother."

"You mean, all this time . . . ? I haven't done anything wrong, Mother. I swear it!"

"I know, Ruth. You were afraid I wouldn't let you see him. I'm sorry you felt that way. In truth, I don't know what I would have said if you had asked me. But . . ." She lifted her hand, let it drop. "That's unimportant now. Is he a good person?"

"He's wonderful, Mother! When the war is over, he plans to be a teacher. He wants to teach high-school mathematics and physics. He's so brilliant. He tells me all sorts of things about the world. . . ."

"Does he love you?"

"Yes!"

"Do you love him?"

"Oh, yes, Mama. He wants to marry me."

"Ruth, oh, Ruth. You are so young."

The siren came on now, as the ambulance slipped between the traffic outside the hospital entrance.

We had arrived. The orderlies rushed to open the ambulance door, to take out the gurney upon which Mother lay. When next we saw her, she had already been prepared for surgery and was nearly asleep.

She reached out her hand, her eyes half-closed. "Annie!"

"Yes, Mama."

"Be a good girl. Do everything your sisters tell you. They will take care of you."

"I will, Mama."

"Lisa!"

"Yes, Mama."

"Don't stop dancing. I mean it!" she said, with sudden strength.

"I'll practice every day. I promise."

"You have a special talent, Lisa."

"I know." I felt the lump in my throat; it was as if she lay dying.

"Arthur!"

"Margo, spare yourself. . . ."

"That new coat, the one with the double row of buttons . . ."

"Yes, yes?"

"I think you should make it in blue, Arthur. Navy blue. It looks, then, like a sailor coat. People will like it. They'll buy it like hotcakes."

"What did you say, Margo?"

"Like hot—hot—" her voice trailed off, and she was sound asleep.

A nurse came in, checked her blood pressure. "Strong medicine," she said. "She's way under."

Papa, half-grinning, yet with tears in his eyes, shook his head, slapped his thigh. "Imagine it! The woman is half-unconscious, she tells me about my latest models, what colors to make. And she is right! She's absolutely right! They'll sell like hotcakes."

That night, after Mama's surgery, I did not know what to do to make myself stop worrying. I returned to my chair and wrote:

March 6, 1943—Saturday. This morning Annie and I cleaned the whole house, and then I took Annie over to the high school and we threw baseballs for an hour or so. We called the hospital, but we could not visit, because Mama just came out of surgery and is very weak. Annie asked me whether Mama could die. I said no. But I am not sure. If she dies, what will I do? How could I stand

it? Annie is so sad. She doesn't make any jokes, and she
hardly talks. She didn't even listen to her radio programs
this morning. If Mama dies, how could I take care of Annie?
I'm scared.

Somehow, for the next week, we made do without Mama.
Until then I had not realized how many things she did for
us every day, or how smoothly the household seemed to
run itself when she was around.

Laundry piled up. Buttons mysteriously fell off our
clothes. Food disappeared, milk soured, the mail and the
newspapers littered windowsills and corners, and nobody
could find anything.

"Where is that black thread? And what happened to
my bankbook?" Papa cried, padding around distractedly,
shaking his head. "Girls, girls, I've lost my little telephone
directory—God, I'm done for!"

We visited Mother in the hospital. Three, four, five days
passed. Mother looked very weak. Where before she had
issued instructions, now she seemed to have slipped into
a kind of twilight place. She nodded when we entered,
but she did not smile or try to talk. "Hello," she would
say listlessly, then she closed her eyes, turning her face
away.

Dr. Belzac met us in the hall.

He said, "The incision is healing as expected." He
sighed. "But I wish she would eat more and regain her
strength."

"She pays no attention when we come to see her,"
Papa said.

Dr. Belzac looked surprised.

"My wife is not herself, Doctor," Papa cried. "She

doesn't talk, doesn't smile. Even when the children come, she looks at the wall. I—I don't know what to do.''

"It will probably pass. Surgery is a shock to the body, you know.''

"What?" Papa cried. "I want my wife back the way she was! I give her to you, you say she must have this operation, and look! The woman is like a ghost, lying still on the bed, a ghost, a ghost!''

"Mr. Platt," said the doctor. "Your wife is depressed. We knew this even before the operation. With the anesthesia and the surgery, loss of blood, everything has come together. Your wife needs rest. Complete rest for a few weeks, and maybe then . . .''

"Maybe!" roared my father. "I don't want 'maybe.' You're the doctor. Make her well!''

A nurse came rushing in, distracted, hands raised, "Sir! Lower your voice. This is a hospital.''

"Then make my wife well!" he shouted. "I need her. She is the mother of these children.''

Dr. Belzac clasped my father by the arm, and I could tell it took all his strength to steer my father farther down the hall, talking to him all the while. "Mr. Platt, I know how it is. I know how you feel. Listen, we must have patience. We will try everything. Your wife is in shock. She has lost hope. Don't you understand?''

"I want her back! I want her back!" From the outer hall we heard Father shouting. Then came silence. Then his cries.

The two men remained out in the hall for a long time. Occasionally we heard a sound, a rumbling, an indistinct word. Later Papa told us what had transpired.

"After the operation," he said, "in the recovery room,

your mother was crying, the doctor said. She was shouting. Arguing.''

"Arguing?" we said, puzzled. "With whom?"

"With God."

I shook my head. "What do you mean?"

"Dr. Belzac says she was blaming Him. For her mother's death. She said, 'You let it happen. How could You? I did everything—I prayed. I helped the poor. I took care of my children. And now, see, how You turn Your face away, letting the innocent die.' "

Papa's face was covered with perspiration. "In the recovery room they said she twisted and turned and fought. She screamed, 'I don't need a God who lets old women and little children be murdered. No more prayers, no more. Don't tell me You are God, and that You will save, that You do justice. It's all lies! I don't believe in You anymore—for me, You are dead.' "

Annie sat there shivering. "She said God is dead?"

"For her," Papa said, his voice trembling. "Yes, for her God is dead."

"And now she won't get well," Annie said. "Because God will punish her."

"No, no," Papa said. He reached out his hands to Annie, held her close for a moment. "God does not punish people who cry out in their grief."

"Then why isn't she getting better?" Annie asked.

"I don't know. Maybe because she has too much anger in her," Papa said. "Too much grief. It must find a way out."

"How, Papa?" I asked.

He shrugged, helpless. "I wish I knew."

Later that evening I went to Papa. He was in the living

room sitting under the lamp, sewing a brown satin lining into a fur collar.

"Isn't it late for you?" he asked.

"I'm not tired," I said.

"Sew a collar then," Papa said. "It will make you tired."

I was already threading a needle. The brown lining was loosely pinned into the underside of the fur. Deftly I folded the satin cloth under and began to make tiny, almost invisible stitches, just barely catching the leather backing with the point of my needle. I had gotten so that I could finish a collar in twenty minutes or so. Mother did it in exactly seventeen minutes.

"I'll sew more now," I told Papa, "to make up for Mother."

"Your schoolwork comes first," he said firmly.

"I know."

"And your mother wants you to dance. How often she tells me this! 'I have not brought these children over to America to see them working in a sweatshop! I want them to be educated. To be somebody.' She has ideas, your mother, big ideas of what she wants for you."

"She always told me," I said, trying to disguise my emotion, "that one shouldn't make bargains with God. That we should pray only in thanks, or to ask God for strength."

My father's brows drew together as he still bent low to his sewing. "So. Maybe your mother did make a bargain with Him. Who can blame her? These are terrible times. We are so helpless. We try to do anything, even making a bargain with God. She lost. Poor woman." He twisted the thread around his finger, tore it off, and took up another fur collar.

"Have you stopped believing in God, too?" I asked.

"I never gave so much thought to Him at all, Lisa. Maybe that is bad. I just always figured I should go about my own business and let God take care of His."

"Do you think He is taking proper care of the world?" I asked, though half-afraid to say the words.

"Well, I don't think you or I could do any better," Papa said, sewing briskly. "It takes all my energy just to make a good wool coat that will sell for less than the competition's."

My name was on the list of those chosen to dance at the Shrine Auditorium.

For days I had dreaded and feared the announcement. Not to be chosen would have been a crushing blow. To be chosen, however, filled me with conflict. Here was my dream within reach, but impossible to grasp.

My friends came with me to see the results. They were ecstatic.

"I told you you'd make it," Sheila cried, hugging me. "I knew it! I'm so proud of you, Lis'."

"You'll be one of the lead dancers," Janine said. "Listen to my prediction. You'll see. This is your big opportunity."

"But I can't accept," I said.

"What?" they cried. "Are you crazy?"

"With my mother sick, I'm needed at home. I have to take care of Annie. And Papa needs me to sew."

"How can you even think about things like that!" Louise exclaimed. "If you really want to be a dancer, you have to forget everything else. Except Elysians, of course." She laughed, then said seriously, "We really want you in the club, Lisa."

I said, "This program isn't enough to make me a dancer. I should be taking lessons outside of school, with a private teacher, someone from the French or the Russian ballet."

"Won't your parents let you take lessons?" asked Louise.

I looked at her in amazement, and with envy, too. Poor Louise—she had no notion at all of my situation. For her, needing money simply meant coaxing her daddy to be more generous.

I pushed back my pride. "We can't afford it," I said. "Especially now, with mother's illness."

"Just don't be hasty," Janine advised. "Maybe something will turn up. Don't say anything yet to the Nazi."

"Don't call her that anymore," I said. "She was fair to me, after all."

When I told Ruth that afternoon she, too, was adamant.

"You have to dance, Lisa," she said. "Mother even told you so, in the ambulance."

"I don't think you realize what Madame will demand. We'll have rehearsals almost every night, certainly every afternoon."

Ruth said, "Listen. I'll take care of Mother. I'm the one who's going to be a nurse. I might as well have the practice."

"But there's Annie to think of, too."

"Annie is old enough to take care of herself."

"And what about you? What about Peter?"

She turned away, went to the window. "Peter is leaving tonight," she said. I heard the tremor in her voice.

"Tonight?"

"He asked me to go with him," Ruth said. "To his home in Michigan. He wanted me to meet his parents. He said we'd go on the train together. We would have been—together."

"What did you tell him? You mean you'd be lovers?"
I could hardly say the word.

"I'm supposed to meet him at the station at six. I was
going to leave Mother and Father a note. After all, these
are the things every person has to decide for himself."

I nodded slightly. I was holding my breath.

"Now I know I can't do it. Mother needs me. I couldn't
leave her. Or the rest of you."

"Ruth, oh, Ruth." I was stunned at the idea of Ruth
going off to meet her lover, like a heroine in the movies,
to go away with him and spend those last nights in his
embrace. How could she not go to him now, if she truly
loved him?

"Stop crying, silly!" she commanded.

I realized my cheeks were wet with tears.

"We've got to get dinner started. There're no clean sheets
in the closet, and Mother's coming home tomorrow." Ruth
stood before me, hands on hips.

"But what about Peter?" I cried. "What will you tell
him?"

"That's *my* problem," Ruth snapped. "Now, go get
Annie. She's got to do her homework. And if she doesn't
do what she's told, I'm going to spank her, hard!"

I found Annie out in the backyard, sitting in the crotch
of the olive tree, reading a comic book.

"You've got to come in," I said. "Get out of that tree.
You have to study."

"I won't," she shouted. "You can't make me."

"Yes, I can. And I will. Ruth and I both. We want
you to get inside and get busy. If you don't get out of
that tree, I'm turning the hose on you."

"You wouldn't!"

"I would."

"Liar!"

I ran for the hose, with the nozzle attached. Full force, I let the water shoot up into the tree, soaking Annie, who clambered down, wrested the hose away, and managed to turn it on me. We screamed and laughed, pushed and sprayed. At last both of us, dripping and gasping, went inside to clean up.

Ruth was nowhere to be seen.

"Ruth," I called, panicked.

No answer. Then I heard a dull sound. She was in the closet off the living room, thumping her foot once against the door to let me know. For privacy, she had taken the telephone into the closet.

Chastened, I went into the kitchen to prepare supper, while Annie sat at the table doing math problems.

After a while I heard Ruth in our small hallway, and I knew she had put back the phone and gone to her room.

We called her to supper.

She called back, "Eat without me. Please."

Much later, after Papa, Annie, and I had eaten and the kitchen was clean, I went to Ruth's room with a glass of milk and a piece of cold chicken.

She was sitting at her little wicker desk, eyes straight ahead, unblinking.

"Ruth," I whispered. "Are you okay?"

"Yes."

"Was that Peter on the phone?"

"Yes."

"What did you tell him?"

"The truth."

"What did he say?"

Ruth sighed. "Lots of things. All private."

"Does he still want to marry you?"

She nodded. "We'll write to each other. I told him, if we really love each other, we don't need those nights to prove it. We'll still love each other when he comes back. I've made another decision," she said.

"What's that?"

"Right after graduation, I'm joining the Cadette Nursing Corps. That means I'll get my training for free, if I promise to join the Corps when I graduate, to be an army nurse."

"An army nurse! Oh, Ruth!"

"Then, if the war is still on, I can at least help."

I nodded. My heart pounded dully. "Ruth, I feel so useless!" I cried. "So unimportant. You're going to be a nurse and heal people, help the war effort, and I'm supposed to pretend everything's normal, and go on dancing, be on the stage . . . How can I?"

Ruth looked at me very seriously. "Mother said you have a talent. She's right. You're supposed to use it. The show is to raise money for war bonds, isn't it? Isn't that what you told me?"

"Yes." Slowly I nodded.

"Then it's your duty to dance. To do whatever you can to help the war effort."

How strange, I thought, that my duty should be to do the very thing I loved most. And yet, I would have to make a sacrifice, too.

Maybe I *was* different from the other girls. I had different ideas. Some of those came from being German, some from being Jewish, and some just from being me. I decided to stop worrying so much about fitting in with everybody else. Oh, I still wanted friends, and I loved being with them. But I also remembered what Mrs. Morgan had said,

about having your own style. In a way, doing what you
need to do is also a matter of style.

All night I thought of it, between dreams. I could not
go on as I'd been doing, trying to be popular, spending
my money on clothes and cosmetics, thinking constantly
about the Elysians and all the plans for dances and parties
and outings.

On the first day of rehearsal came another blow.

"Your costumes will be designed and made for you by
a professional costumer," said Madame Klausenstock, bark-
ing out the words. "Your measurements will be taken on
Friday. The costumes cost fourteen dollars each. Also, each
of you will need new toe shoes. And a specially designed
rhinestone tiara. The total cost will be twenty-eight dollars.
You are to bring the money, in the form of a check or
money order, to school on Friday. Is that clear?"

Nobody said anything. After rehearsal the girls clustered
together, appalled, and finally acquiescent.

"How dare she?"

"Who has twenty-eight dollars?"

"My parents won't mind—but the nerve!"

"Well, we don't have any choice. We have to have
costumes."

"Twenty-eight dollars! That will take all my birthday
money."

I sighed. Now, I thought, I didn't have to worry anymore
about how to spend the money in my bank account.

The next day I went to the bank and withdrew twenty-
eight dollars in a cashier's check, and took seven dollars
in cash. Twenty remained in the account. Twenty dollars
would buy me four or five lessons with a good dance teacher.
Meanwhile, I'd work for Papa and at the bakery to pay

for more lessons. It was time, I knew, to invest in my future.

My friends would have to understand; I couldn't join the club. I just wasn't meant to be an Elysian, to live in a mythical place like that, where the pleasures of paradise are given on a silver platter.

With the seven dollars I went to Robinson's, where I bought Mother a beautiful peach-colored satin bed jacket with tiny roses embroidered on the collar. I had hoped to buy a farewell gift for Will. I decided, instead, to knit socks and send them to him. Meanwhile, I searched through our pictures and selected a photograph of the three of us sitting together on a park bench. On the back of it I wrote, "With love from your friends, Ruth, Lisa, and Annie Platt." He was leaving in a week.

Chapter 17

CHARLOTTA GOT THE USE of her father's car. She came driving up to get Ruth and me.

"How's your mother?" she shouted.

"Resting," Ruth said. Ruth had left Annie in charge of her patient. Father was packing a shipment of coats out in the garage.

"What's wrong with her?" Charlotta asked, gunning the motor. Ruth and I settled back, I holding onto the dashboard as Charlotta sped off.

"Nervous depression," I said.

Ruth gave me a poke. "Recovering from surgery," she said.

Both were true. Mother had been home for nearly a week with no real improvement. We turned on the radio for her, thinking she'd love to hear the soap operas, "Helen Trent" and "Young Doctor Malone."

"Turn that off!" she'd cry. "Why do you want to irritate me?"

Annie came to read to her. Mother waved her away. "Go out and play. Get fresh air. Don't sit here, Annie. I don't need anything."

Whatever it was she needed, we couldn't provide it. Papa sat with her by the hour. He brought in the newspaper to read beside her. From the delicatessen he bought specialties—stuffed cabbage and German dishes. Nothing helped. I felt guilty. I was gone most of the time at rehearsals. Even today, Sunday, we were expected at the gym by two in the afternoon.

"I hear you are getting into the theater," Charlotta yelled to me over the roar of the motor.

"Not exactly," I shouted back. "I'm only dancing in a bond program."

"You'll show those Americans what we're made of," Charlotta exclaimed. "The best actresses and dancers in the world are from Europe. Hard workers! Talented."

I thought of Ginger Rogers and all the other American stars, who were also hard workers and talented. I said nothing.

"Tony asked me for my picture in a bathing suit," Charlotta yelled. "He wants to put it up in his barracks, he said. Instead of Betty Grable. It's in the glove box. Take a look."

We took out the picture. A large print of Charlotta in a knitted bathing suit showed more flesh than we'd ever seen in public.

"Like it?" shouted Charlotta.

My face burned.

"Tony will like it," Ruth said. "That's what counts."

"We're secretly engaged," Charlotta said.

Ruth and I exchanged glances. We knew what that meant; they had slept together.

Ruth sighed.

I felt like a child beside them. And then we arrived at Union Station, that bustling, noisy, cold, and impersonal place with the sleek, dark floors and huge pillars, carved ceiling and long benches. And everywhere, everywhere the clustered knots of people, mothers and fathers trying to look casual, young women with freshly washed hair and new clothes, smiling hard, making themselves beautiful for that last look they would give to their boyfriends, for who could say how very long? We heard the cold clattering of iron doors, the groaning and churning of the trains. The sound of the train struck terror into my heart; we had taken such a train out of Berlin, narrowly escaping the Nazis. I would never in my life be near a train without remembering that.

And suddenly our attention was pulled to the groups of young men, all trotting out in formation, the first steps into war.

"There's Will!" I shouted.

Each company gathered under a sign with its commander; already the boys looked different. Their faces had a certain sameness about them, as if they were cut out of cardboard, eyes unflinching, jaws taut. They were a unit now, not individuals; as a unit they moved, followed orders. As a unit, they would kill. It was the first moment I actually realized it; they were going overseas to kill people. Or to be killed.

Will waved to us. "Hello, hello, girls," he shouted.

His mother and sisters were there.

"Hi, Will," we called. What else could we say?

Small talk erupted; silly nonsense. "My mother packed up a whole tin of cookies! Thinks I'll starve in the army!"

"My dad says when he was in the service he gained twenty pounds."

"My pop was over in France in the big war. Spent four months in a trench."

The boys smoked. It gave them something to do, tapping out their cigarettes, lighting up, exhaling.

"Company—all aboard!" came the shout.

All over the world, I thought, young men were boarding trains and ships and planes, so that they might soon meet, in combat. A sailor limped past on crutches. His uniform was spotless. The left trouser leg was pinned up at the knee. I felt dizzy and wanted to hold on to Ruth, but I didn't. I knew him! I wanted to shout his name, but I couldn't catch my breath.

"Lester, Lester!" Ruth screamed.

"Lester!" I shouted, turning as he saw us and came limping over to clasp me in his arms as he repeated, "The Platt girls! Oh, my God, it's the Platt girls!"

We had only a few moments. We screamed out our information, the few most significant facts telescoped from the events of over two years. I tried not to stare at Lester's crutches as he told us he had been hospitalized in San Diego for the past five months, was visiting some buddies in Anaheim, and was bound now for home.

"So tell me about you all!"

As we hurriedly spoke, I realized that in spite of everything, life had gone on for us more or less routinely, and pleasantly.

"How's Annie?"

"Great. She plays baseball. A real tomboy."

"And your pa?"

"Doing fine, selling coats."

"And your mother?"

"She's been sick. She'll be okay."

"You girls look great! Lisa, you're so American." Lester reached out, took my arms and hugged me.

"Thanks," I said, laughing. "You look terrific, too." And he did—taller, broader, his jaw set firmly, almost handsome.

"What will you do now?" Ruth asked.

"Uncle Sam's sending me to college," he said. "All expenses paid. I'm going to study engineering."

"How are your folks?" we asked.

Lester shrugged. "Mom's okay. My pa died. Construction accident."

"Oh! I'm sorry," I said.

"I've got to go, Lisa. Take care of yourselves."

"You, too. You, too," we cried.

Suddenly he was gone, and I could feel the movement of crowds, and then Will and Tony, Gary and Richard were saying the last-minute awkward words to their families while Ruth and I just stood there. This was the parting I'd prepared for a hundred times in my mind. Now, I was unprepared.

"Good-bye, Lisa." Will leaned toward me. Gently he touched his lips to mine.

I handed him the envelope with the photograph inside.

He kissed Ruth, exactly as he had me. "Thanks for the memories," Will said, using the words of a popular song.

"Okay," said Ruth, blushing.

Will's mother began to cry, biting her lips in a useless effort to disguise it.

"All aboard!"

Wheels churned, steam hissed out. The engines broke through the noise of our voices.

On the way home, none of us had much to say.

I had Charlotta leave me off at school. I rushed to the gym to be in time for rehearsal.

"Smile, smile, smile," shouted Madame Klausenstock as she put us through our paces, beating her stick in time to the routine. "No, no, no," she shouted when we missed a beat. "Pay attention. What's the matter with all of you? We'll stay here until you get it right. *Get it right*. Lisa Platt, for God's sake, get your mind on the dance. And smile. You look like your bones are breaking. Smile!"

Dr. Belzac came to the house to see Mother. He ordered her to get out of bed for an hour each morning and again in the afternoon. "And to the table for dinner with your family," he said briskly. "Mrs. Platt, you must make the effort. Please."

"Very well. If you say so." Mother closed her eyes.

"And open your eyes, Mrs. Platt. Ah. Lovely blue eyes like these should be open for people to see."

Mother did not even smile.

"I hear you are an excellent baby nurse, Mrs. Platt. Trained in Europe."

"Yes," Mother said. She looked up at him for the first time.

"I have a baby at home. My wife has been staying home with her, but she wants to get back to work, too. It's a little girl."

"A girl!" Mother whispered.

The doctor took a photograph from his pocket and showed it to her.

Mother looked at the picture for a long moment. "What is her name?" she asked.

"Daphne."

"What a beautiful name!" Mother exclaimed. "What a lovely child." The next moment she lay back, as if even this small effort had exhausted her.

Later Dr. Belzac and Father stood in the driveway talking together.

I went back to Mother's room.

She lay in the bed, weeping. "Mother!" I rushed to her side. She pushed me away. I ran out to call Papa.

"Mother's crying!"

Dr. Belzac put up his hand. "That's not bad," he said. "Not bad at all. It shows that your mother is allowing herself to feel again. She is returning. Slowly, yes, but I think that seeing this baby has helped her somehow. Let us hope so."

Four days later a letter came from Germany. The black swastika on the envelope was a hateful intrusion into our home.

I was just back from rehearsal, and I ran with the letter out to the garage, to Papa.

He came in at once, opening the letter carefully in the kitchen with a knife. He unfolded the page. Only two words had been blotted out in black. Swiftly Father read, then he paced.

"I don't know what to do," he said. "I don't know whether to show this to your mother."

"Who's it from?"

"Clara." He handed me the letter, and I read:

> *My dear Mrs. Platt,*
> *A thousand thanks for your wonderful parcel.*
> *Everything in it is precious to us.*

*My heart grieves over the news I must give
you. Your dear mother has gone on a long journey. You must believe me when I tell you I did
all I could to prevent the departure. Alas, what
can we do? Our hands are tied by the events
here. It is too late to stop them now. You know
I would do anything on earth if I could help
you in this hour of your loss, my dear friend.
All any of us can do is to raise our prayers to
the Almighty. He alone sees beyond this terrible
storm to the ultimate victory over the—(here two
words were blotted out)—who will surely perish.
I know and believe this with perfect faith. I thank
God for your safety in America. You now hold
the torch for all of us here. We shall never lose
faith in you.*

> *Your devoted,*
> *Clara*

I said, "How could Clara have sent such a letter out?
She should be afraid of what they might do. The Nazis
read all the mail."

Papa nodded. "I know. It is very dangerous for her."

"She said she *believes*!"

I saw tears in Papa's eyes. "I'm afraid I have let us
wander too far away from our beginnings," Papa murmured.
"We must find our way back."

"Back? To the past?"

"No," Papa said. "But our future must have room in
it for the past. For the good things from the past. Like
faith. Clara lives by her faith. What an inspiration! Writing
that letter took courage."

"What took courage?" Suddenly Mother stood there at the kitchen door in her nightgown. "What?"

Papa hesitated, then nodded to me.

I handed Mother the letter.

She read it once, then again. She looked at me and Papa. "What a woman," she said. She took the letter with her into the bedroom.

We crept about the house, afraid. Some time later Mother emerged. Her hair was pinned up. She wore a clean housedress.

A short time later we five sat down together at the diningroom table for the first time in weeks.

"It's Friday," I suddenly said, realizing it.

Papa gazed at me, then nodded.

"Wait," I said to everyone. "Please, wait a minute."

Out in the kitchen, far back in the high cupboard, were the few remaining glass-star ashtrays left over from Papa's venture. Quickly I pulled up a chair, climbed it and got down two of the stars, and inserted two white candles that Mama kept in the drawer for air-raid emergencies.

I brought the candles to the table, along with a box of matches.

"Mother," I said softly, "let's light the candles. It's Sabbath."

Slowly my mother rose. She picked up her cloth napkin and placed it on her head, as she had always done in the old days, as Jewish women have done through the ages, respecting God.

Mother struck the match. Carefully she lit one candle, then the other, and made the slow circling motions over the flames as she prayed:

"*Baruch atta Adonay, Elohaynu, melech h'olam . . .*"

"Praised art Thou, oh Lord, our God, king of the universe . . ."

Mother looked at me, smiling. *"Shabbat Shalom."* Sabbath peace.

"Peace," we murmured, all together, and we watched the candles for a long moment, letting the echo of that word settle upon us.

Epilogue

MOTHER RECOVERED QUICKLY after that. Dr. Belzac begged her to come to his house and care for his baby girl. Mother was overjoyed. She loved the baby and regained her strength.

At the bond-drive show, I danced in the front row. I was third from the left. Nobody discovered me. Nobody asked me to dance in the movies. But my friends came and applauded wildly, and the show raised seventy-thousand dollars in three weeks. When at last the war was over and the boys came marching home, I knew I'd done my small share. I was a real American.